THE WOMEN ON THE ISLAND

THE WOMEN ON THE ISLAND

A NOVEL

by Ho Anh Thai

Translated by
Phan Thanh Hao,
Celeste Bacchi,
and Wayne Karlin

Introduction by
Wayne Karlin

University of Washington Press
Seattle and London

Originally published in Vietnam as *Nguoi dan ba tren dao*
by N.x.b., Lao Dong, Ha Noi (Labor Publishing House),
Ha Noi, 1988

Printed in the United States of America

ISBN 0-295-98086-9 (cloth)
ISBN 0-295-98108-3 (paperback)

The paper used in this publication is acid-free and recycled from 10 percent post-consumer and at least 50 percent pre-consumer waste. It meets the minimum requirements of American National Standard for Information Sciences—Permanence of Paper for Printed Library Materials, ANSI Z39.48-1984. ∞ ♻

INTRODUCTION

Ho Anh Thai is one of the most prolific writers in Vietnam. An army veteran, a diplomat who has served abroad and who is now an editor for the foreign service journal *World Affairs Weekly,* he has managed to produce fifteen novels and story collections as well as hundreds of short stories, and has edited both an anthology of translated Vietnamese stories published in India and an anthology of translated contemporary American fiction published in Vietnam. His first story, written when he was seventeen years old, drew national attention. The editors who accepted it for one of the leading literary journals in Vietnam presumed he was a much older, mature writer and were astonished when the slim teenager showed up at their offices. A compulsive, voracious reader since childhood, Thai had come early to the conclusion that he could write as well as, or better than, the authors of the stories and novels he picked up. He would not imitate, he decided, but create his own path. It is this mindset that has made him one of the most popular writers for the post-war generation in Vietnam—the generation that was too young to fight, but that grew up with the sound and fury of the war in their ears and eyes, with the heroics and sacrifices of their parents' generation as an ideal almost impossible to follow, and with the promise of a prosperous and peaceful postwar society seemingly out of their grasp.

Born in Hanoi in 1960, Thai and thousands of other children his age were evacuated to a "safe" area in the countryside when the American bombing campaign began. The war followed him there: one of his earliest memories is of swimming with a group of kids from Hanoi and from the village where the city children had been sent, and suddenly seeing the American planes bombing the village, then running back with a friend, a young girl, to find the house where her parents were staying destroyed and still burning. The image was seared into his eyes, and can perhaps stand for the way the tremendous losses of the war generation continue to haunt subsequent generations in Vietnam. Three million Vietnamese died in the war with the Americans, countless more were wounded, missing, poisoned by chemicals, traumatized. Hundreds of thousands had given up any hope of individual happiness in order to achieve victory. It is always difficult for the children of heroes and martyrs to find their own identities, and it is particularly so when they grow up in a country whose severe deprivations, themselves a result of the war, seem to call into question the values and methods of their elders. That struggle illuminates much of Ho Anh Thai's work. To define themselves and their direction, he suggests, the postwar generations must be able to concede their debt to the past, but also to see clearly what must be criticized and changed: they must build on the past rather than remain in it. That perception is not only stressed thematically in Thai's work, he also applies it through his play and experimentation with form and language. He acknowledges with respect and love his roots in the history and literature of his country, but has also been open to other influences—notably Latin American magic realism, and the work of the Czech writer Milan Kundera—and he has allowed his own writing to extend contemporary Vietnamese literature into new directions. The title novella of his collection *Behind the Red Mist,* published in the United States in 1998, serves as an example of Thai's daring as a writer, and illustrates the themes that he explores in much of his work.

A fantasy, the novel takes a modern Hanoi youth of Thai's generation, and by means of an electric shock (received when a building whose war-time foundations were poorly built collapses) sends him back in time, to the Hanoi of the war, where he witnesses and participates in the courtship of his own parents. In discovering the humanity of his parents, the ways they were like him in their youth, he also finds the humanity of that venerated, mythological war-time generation—discovers its flaws as well as its strength and courage. In doing so, he makes himself (and symbolically his generation) a part of it, part of the ongoing flow of Vietnamese history. That use of very real characters put into fantastical situations in order to shake the truth out of perception, marks much of Thai's writing. But it is also marked by a kind of gentle whimsy and tenderness. Ho Anh Thai is a writer with few illusions about human beings, and maybe even little hope. But in spite of, or perhaps because of that, he treats his characters with a compassion which reveals his respect for the complexity of their humanity.

The Women on the Island is set in the mid 1980s, when Vietnam was just entering the consumer society which, for better and worse, has since become the norm and made the heroism of the war generation passé. The novel opens a window onto a culture struggling to define its relationship to its own past and to its future. The tension between efficient and daring younger people who challenge the laziness and corruption of entrenched officials and bureaucrats is a theme often depicted in the work of Vietnamese writers after the policy of *doi moi,* renovation, was initiated in 1986 to open the free market system in Vietnam. The character of Hoa, the young director of a state-owned export company in the New Economic Zone of Cat Bac Island—his competence, his sense of fairness, his willingness to forget past crimes and weaknesses in the name of effectiveness and productivity, epitomizes the *doi moi* version of the Ideal Man: no longer Socialist Man but rather Socialist Man in the Free Market: courageous, intelligent, personally ambitious yet socially responsible, and always in control. Yet Hoa finds his own exemplar in Mr. Chinh, a figure who, according to the Vietnam scholar Neil Jamieson, represents the Zen virtues of calmness and detachment that marked Vietnamese culture in the Ly dynasty, a millennium ago. The original title of the novel, in fact, was *Keep Sharpening the Whip,* a reference to Mr. Chinh's gentle means of getting rid of anger by whittling down the bamboo he would use for a whip until it disappears.* Hoa looks to Mr. Chinh's example as a way he can use those ancient strengths to deal with the vicissitudes of the modern world.

Some of those vicissitudes reveal the tensions besetting the Vietnamese economy during the time-setting of the novel. Both Hoa's export company, and the forestry enterprise in which the "women on the island" toil, are commonly known as "state-owned enterprises" (SOEs). Besides the companies mentioned in the novel, SOEs can also be hotels, stores, entertainment complexes, tourist services, and (now) even internet servers. Jamieson notes that in the mid-eighties, before *doi moi* encouraged free market enterprise, there were approximately 12,000 SOEs in Vietnam. Post *doi moi,* that number has been cut in half. Some of the problems endemic in SOEs are epitomized in such incidents as the pathetic Quy receiving a position because of his uncle's influence, the carelessness in packing goods for shipment that costs so much to the export company, the general disregard for and despoliation of natural resources, the brutal use of public criticism and shaming which was common until the late 1980s, and the petty struggles for power seen when an official tries to blame his rival for the pregnancy of one of the girls in the production brigade.

*Neil Jamieson, communication to the translators, February 17, 2000. The second Vietnamese printing of the novel in 1996 came out under the title of *Keep Sharpening the Whip,* although the author has said that the next will once again be *The Women on the Island*.

These glimpses of the social tensions that have beset postwar Vietnam are interesting and informative for the Western reader, and reflect problems in much of the world as it moves into a global economy. But what elevates *The Women on the Island* to a more universal exploration of the human condition is its exploration of an elemental human conflict. While Hoa's fight against corruption and inefficiency plays an important part in the novel, it is his struggle against his own nature which saves him from being as one-dimensional a character as the noble proletarian heroes who are his literary predecessors. Another central character, Tuong, the fallen man, the randy artist, may express many readers' reaction to Hoa's unrelenting virtue, after Hoa tells him he regards all women as either mothers or sisters: "As he looked into Hoa's clear eyes and sincere face, he thought . . . Fine. Let him be a saint. But did he have to impose his ideas of chastity on other people? Did he have to try to extinguish everyone else's sexual desires?" In fact, what becomes interesting in Hoa's personality are the cracks, the sexuality he can't (at least for a while) control or deny. It is that battle, waged to one extent or another within many of the characters, which makes *The Women on the Island* unique and daring among renovation fiction in Vietnam.

Sexuality becomes in the novel a symbol of all the messy complications of the human personality, the human needs which can't be conveniently defined, controlled, subordinated, simplified to a pure ideal, whether that ideal be revolution, war, social justice, or business success.

Ho Anh Thai begins *The Women on the Island* with a fable-like story about a band of guerillas fighting the French, which serves as a brilliant coda for the novel. Their leader, General Tan Dac, "regarded as a father, and almost as a god," is infuriated when some of his men rape a woman, and orders their beheading. Tan Dac tells his men that they must think only of the struggle for freedom: "they had only one right: to defeat the enemy. All personal desires, all other needs and hungers, had to be eliminated." The young men obey, but when they stop a farmer and find some jackfruit and bamboo in his bag, they are so driven by what they've suppressed that they're convinced these stand for "the male sexual organ" and that he is trying to torment or subvert them. The man is beheaded also, but his blood soaks into the earth, and the scattered seeds of the jackfruit and bamboo grow into the fecund jungle on the island that becomes the setting for the modern story.

The guerillas are ultimately replaced in that same jungle, in the 1980s, by Production Brigade Five, a company of women who become both their inheritors and the true center of the novel. The women, most of them veterans of the war, have been sent there to work in a state forestry enterprise to help in the area's economic development. In focusing on them, Ho Anh Thai became one of the first writers in Vietnam to bring attention to what had been a forbidden subject: the terrible cost paid by Vietnamese women who were veterans of the American War. During the war, tens of thousands of young women and girls served both as fighters with the Southern guerillas (and to a lesser extent with the Army of the Republic of Vietnam), and in other support roles. Thousands of young women (fifteen years old and up) in the North joined the Volunteer Youth Corps of the People's Army of Vietnam. Their main duties during the war were to keep the Ho Chi Minh Trail network open, to fill in bomb craters, repair roads, and defuse or explode unexploded bombs. Though many were city girls, they endured unimaginable hardships with great courage, living for years in the jungles and in caves, starving, subject to lice, snakebite, and disease, and dying by the thousands in bombing and strafing attacks. In an interview with Karen Turner, Le Minh Khue, a writer who served as a Volunteer Youth for five years, gives an example both of the type of horror endured and the way women were called upon to participate in what had been for the most part traditionally male activities:

> Men bury the dead in peacetime. During the war, women had to do it. They would get up . . . bury the day's dead, make the coffins, and dig the burial trenches . . . sometimes the burial trenches were bombed and they had to take the bodies out and rebury them. Some bodies were in pieces, some had exploded like bombs from the pressure. It was bad luck for everyone. No, they didn't complain. They had to do it . . . . We had no idea when we signed on how life would be.

Like their counterparts, the male veterans in America and Vietnam, those who survived returned to a society which they had defended, yet which in many ways had no place for them. Many were past the conventional age of marriage, and others had lost their ability to bear children due to exposure to Agent Orange and/or the conditions under which they'd been living. The country's economy, ecology, and infrastructure were in ruins, and the war had decimated the generation of men from which, in other times, they would have found husbands and assumed the traditional place of wife and mother in Vietnamese society. Hundreds of thousands of men in their age group had been killed, wounded physically or psychologically or both, or were already married.

Often then, as is the case with Production Brigade Five, the women were kept together and sent as work teams to the "New Economic Zones," under-populated or devastated areas the government was trying to develop. Such places were even more devoid of eligible men: in the novel, the authorities try at one point to encourage romances between the soldiers in a unit stationed in the area and the women in the production brigade, but the soldiers are of the younger generation and call the women "aunts." Many stories circulated after the war about women in such circumstances who would find whatever men were available and use them to get impregnated, and in fact there were so many cases of single women in these groups becoming pregnant that, according to Phan Thanh Hao, one of the translators of this novel, in 1985 the Vietnamese Women's Union instigated a law making it illegal to harass or ostracize such women and their offspring.

We see such a scene played out in the novel when a callous Party cadre brutalizes a pregnant woman in Production Brigade Five to identify the father of her unborn child: he suspects the guilty party is a political rival and is looking for ammunition with which to attack him. The women, who feel empowered by their military service, rebel against their comrade's treatment:

> They'd survived bombs and bullets, jungle rains and rugged mountains, and they'd risked their lives to do whatever had been asked of them, from building roads to shooting down American aircraft. Their experiences had taught them to obey orders, but their experiences also taught them not to follow the wrong-headed caprices of a dictatorial, hateful bully.

The women's struggle—with their society and within themselves—at first seems to parallel, and indeed is informed by, the struggle with their own natures we saw in Tan Dac's guerillas. Yet while the women are depicted as frustrated in having to repress their normal sexual desires, what they seem mainly to speak of is the desire for motherhood. Tuong the artist, the only virile male available for the women on the island, maintains a calendar in his room marked with the most auspicious dates for intercourse in order to determine the sex of the child: he knows what the women want is not solely sexual release. Part of their motivation surely stems from cultural pressure: For a woman, to be single and childless in traditional Vietnamese society is to be a non-person. Yet while a need for the normalcy of social convention is understandable, for the women in Production Brigade Five the desire for motherhood seems even more motivated by a need for individual fulfillment. The social contract they entered into when they volunteered for the war has failed them, and only a child can provide the truest and most precious and trustworthy companionship. As the brigade leader Mien says:

> We have peace now, but the men we were waiting for never returned. During the American War we lived at the edge of death, and we were able to control our instinctual desires. But now such control is impossible. I know I lost my opportunity to get married. But if at least I had a child, I would be consoled in many ways. If I hadn't been so concerned with "preserving" myself all those years ago, at least I could have had a child with my beloved. And at least I wouldn't have to suffer like I do now. But he's dead, with all the rest, and who did I keep myself for? What do I need with my virginity, when all it does is bring me loneliness? The collective can help me strengthen my willpower, it can console me a bit. But the collective can't bring me private happiness.

It is that need for "private happiness" (even if it takes the outward form of social or peer acceptance) that finally informs the motivations of all the characters. During the war, the struggle, love for the group, the country, the cause, was all and was enough: the individual was subsumed into the national will. But to continue to act that way in a competitive consumer society, with its huge gaps between rich and poor, is to feel like a fool. Sexuality, human nature, the need for individual fulfillment and love, can only be temporarily repressed, but will always emerge again. Like the jackfruit and bamboo that grow from the seed scattered by Tan Dac's men, like the

Vietnamese people themselves, "their life force is a strength nothing can stop."

To deny that force, Ho Anh Thai implies, is both blind and destructive of the individual and of the society in which the individual must live. Yet to live only for its indulgence can be equally disastrous. The questions he and the novel ultimately ask us to consider, then, are the perennial questions literature must always ask: how do we find ways to live in harmony with each other, and within ourselves—with the complex and contradictory compulsions of our own souls?

ACKNOWLEDGMENTS

My gratitude for information about the Youth Volunteer Corps to Karen Gottschang Turner and Phan Thanh Hao and their invaluable book *Even the Women Must Fight: Memories of War From North Vietnam,* and to my friend, the writer Le Minh Khue, who was one of those brave young women.

A NOTE ON THE TRANSLATION

A reader literate in Vietnamese, and with access to a Vietnamese edition, might notice that in a few cases there were changes of sequence and some additions to certain passages in the original text. This was done to provide what we felt was necessary background information to help the reader unfamiliar with Vietnam today. The information was taken from details found elsewhere in the novel, and the basic meaning of the passages was not changed. There are a number of schools of thought about translation. One holds that the original text should be strictly adhered to. There are legitimate reasons to hold such a view, particularly if one's main interest is to perceive how the book was presented to the society in which it was published. It seems to me, though, that such interest is more sociological and cultural than literary. I approached the translation of Ho Anh Thai's novel as an editor whose job was not to change any of the writer's ideas or meanings, but to put them into language which brings them most vividly to a readership different from the one for whom the novel was originally intended. This was done with the complete collaboration of the author and, additionally, with the collaboration of the chief translator in Vietnam, Phan Thanh Hao. We went back and forth on any suggested changes or additions, and never included any until and unless the author approved. The book you have in your hands is very much Ho Anh Thai's book, and very much a living novel.

WAYNE KARLIN

May 2000

THE WOMEN ON THE ISLAND

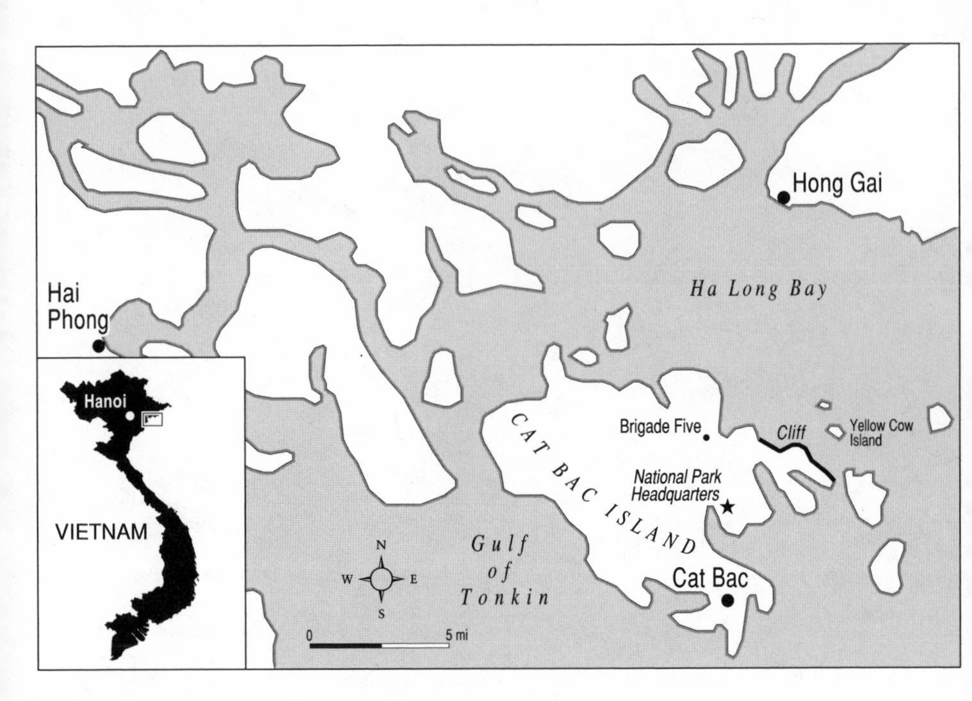

Hong Gai
Ha Long Bay
Hai Phong
Hanoi
VIETNAM
CAT BAC ISLAND
Brigade Five
Cliff
Yellow Cow Island
National Park Headquarters
Cat Bac
Gulf of Tonkin
N
W
E
S
0
5 mi

ONE

In this particular state forestry enterprise on an island off the northeastern coast of Vietnam where nearly 90 percent of the workers are single women, there is not one person who is unaware of the legend of Tan Dac.

It goes like this. Tan Dac was a courageous general under the command of Tan Thuat.* The general was famous for his lightning-like attacks against the French colonialists. When Tan Thuat's insurrection was finally defeated, Tan Dac led the tattered remnants of his guerilla group to Cat Bac Island. They established a base camp near the passage to the northeastern coast, and from there destroyed many of the enemy's ships. The guerillas were young, healthy, and strong, and hatred for the French invaders boiled in their hearts and strengthened their determination to seek revenge for Tan Thuat. They slipped through the jungles and over the mountains, set ambushes and booby traps on the slopes, and lured ships into the mouth of the river. They suffered hunger and cold with patience and

*Nguyen Thien Thuat led an insurrection against the French in the north of Vietnam, 1885–1889.

they were more than willing to sacrifice themselves for their cause. Tan Dac was pleased with his men, and they regarded him as a father and almost as a god.

Then one day near the village of Viet Hoa, Tan Dac came upon an old woman and her daughter. The old woman was on her knees gnawing and tearing at the grass and trying to push her daughter's face into the earth. Seeing her supplicant's posture, Tan Dac asked her to come closer and tell him what was wrong. He was surprised and then enraged to discover that the woman's daughter had been raped by three of his guerillas. In front of the two women and the whole band, the three disgraced men were beheaded. Their unlucky heads rolled on the ground, leaving three lines of blood, like red snakes. Tan Dac wanted to be sure his guerillas understood that they had only one right: to defeat the enemy. All personal desires, all other needs and hungers, had to be eliminated.

The remaining guerillas obeyed their leader without hesitation or reservation. They continued to suffer hunger and cold, and tried desperately to stifle the normal sexual desires of young men. And in reality, in the jungle and mountains of this island, it was rare to encounter anyone who could stir such desire.

It wasn't long after the beheadings when the guerillas came across an old man on his way to pick bamboo shoots. He was carrying a large, bulging jute-fabric bag, which he offered to Tan Dac's men. Ca Dinh, one of Tan Dac's lieutenants, opened the bag and looked inside. His face grew pale. He let the bag drop to the ground, then roared, "Betrayed! Betrayed!"

"What do you mean?" Tan Dac peered inside the bag, shocked at his friend's reaction.

"My dear sir." Ca Dinh trembled with anger as he leaned over to whisper into Tan Dac's ear. "My dear sir, don't you see what's in this bag?"

Without looking again, Tan Dac said, "All I saw were two jackfruits and a bamboo shoot."

"Exactly. Two jackfruits and a bamboo shoot. They signify the male organ, sir."

It is said that the roar that burst from Tan Dac's throat then echoed among the trees and shook their branches. He ordered his men to chase down the old man. They caught him by Red Fish Lake. Without a word, Tan Dac drew his sword and struck through the old man's neck as easily as if he were slashing at the wind. The old man's head flew in one direction, and his poor body fell down near the edge of the lake, dyeing the foam at the water's fringe a deep red. The two jackfruits and the bamboo shoot were thrown down on the bank next to the body. Boiling with anger and humiliation, pushed by their own stifled, thwarted desires, the men rushed upon the fruit and the bamboo and chopped and tore into them, smashing them, slicing open the jackfruit and tearing out its seeds, which were strewn all over the lakeshore like coins. In their hearts, the guerillas could only hold their hatred and their need for revenge. As Tan Dac had told them, all other hopes, sentiments, and desires had to be killed.

The unfortunate old man's children and grandchildren soon heard the terrible news. They took up their spears and their guns and cut their way through the jungle to chase the gueril-las. Ironically, destiny led the two groups to come face to face by Red Fish Lake. Again, there was bloody fighting between two unequal forces. Again bodies were slashed and mutilated. By the end of the battle, only two of the old man's grandchil-dren were left alive. One escaped, but the other was captured and led to Tan Dac. He smiled at the young man and said, "Don't you understand that we're fulfilling our duty to the country by doing our best to kill the French?"

"Yes, I know."

"Aren't you ashamed of losing your country to the French? Join us, and you can wash away your shame."

"It wasn't the French who destroyed my family," the young man said stubbornly. He looked straight ahead, his gaze un-blinking. "Who will avenge them?"

He shared the same fate as his grandfather. His body too was thrown into Red Fish Lake. Soon the brackish water of that lake was said to be cursed with blood. When the weather turned cold, schools of red fish swarmed up and covered the surface of the water like a red sail. In the eyes of the locals, this was the innocent blood of the unjustly killed, blood which couldn't be separated from the water, no matter how many seasons it froze or melted.

The surviving grandson sought vengeance for his family by becoming a scout for the French. Day after day, month after month, he led the blue-eyed, big-nosed foreigners through the jungle, in their hunt for Tan Dac and his guerillas. Eventu-ally, the last surviving members of the band were found hiding in a cave. They were trapped, but steadfastly refused to surrender. After several months, believing that finally all of the guerillas must be dead, the French sealed the entrance of the cave and withdrew.

From that day, no one heard any more about Tan Dac and his guerillas.

But around Red Fish Lake, a large number of jackfruit trees appeared—a forest of jackfruit trees. The fruits ripened and became food for the birds and fell and were scattered. In the season of jackfruit, whoever dared climb up the mountain through the jungle to gather fruit would become drunk from their thick, suffocating smell. And not far from the jackfruit trees had sprung up a thick forest of bamboo. The bamboo shoots grew everywhere, their life force a strength nothing could stop.

❧

Some ninety years later, when the state forestry enterprise was established, Production Brigade Five, which was responsible for planting elshotria pantrine trees and processing the *huong nhu* extract from them,* was settled in Viet Hoa. There were thirty-eight women in Brigade Five, ranging in age from twenty-one to forty-four. Many of them had been in the Volunteer Youth Corps, working on the Ho Chi Minh Trails, but when peace came, there were too few men, and no place in the cities and villages they had left so long ago, for these leftovers from the war, many of them now past the age of

*A type of peppermint oil used to relieve pain.

marriage. Of the group, only Tham was lucky enough to find a husband. Cuong was one of the original inhabitants left in the village, and he worked now as a storage keeper for the forestry collective. None of the women dared to make their way through the jungle and climb up to Red Fish Lake, with its notorious jackfruit trees and groves of bamboo. But the jackfruit trees kept bearing their fruit and the bamboo shoots grew thick and wild and without restraint, like a secret everyone knew and whispered about. Though they had never been there, the image of that forest of jackfruit trees, those bamboo shoots standing upright in their groves, appeared many times to the isolated women, often more clearly and concretely than any images of men they would try to conjure for themselves. Then unexpected good fortune struck one other woman in Brigade Five. Nha was only twenty-one years old, one of the team's youngest members. She'd been on her way to pick up some equipment at the headquarters of the collective, when she suddenly came upon a regiment of soldiers building a road across the island. She was spotted at the same time by Khanh, a regiment scout, and it was this way that the two young people met. Soon after, one Sunday morning, all of Brigade Five was thrown into an uproar over the news that a young man was coming to visit them.

From Khanh's unit to the state forestry enterprise headquarters was a half-hour walk, and from headquarters it took another three hours through the jungle to Viet Hoa. The women were touched and thrilled by Khanh's dedication to Nha. When he arrived, they surrounded him, shooting so many questions at him that he could hardly answer. When he sat down to eat, a frenzy of chopsticks danced around him, piling the food in his rice bowl into a Himalayan peak. Khanh tasted the exquisite suffering of one who is loved by everyone. And when Nha visited his regiment, she met the same fate.

Once the love between these two became known, the board of directors of the state forestry enterprise decided to have a talk with the regimental commander. They confronted frankly the question of how to encourage more bonds between the women in the collective and the soldiers. Such a "love project," they reasoned, would lead to marriages, which meant that many soldiers would volunteer to stay and work on the island after their conscription. Finally, they agreed on a course of action. The regiment would often send several companies to cut timber and bamboo for the forestry collective. In addition, the commander would encourage his soldiers to spend their Sundays off visiting the state forestry enterprise.

The results of the "love project," however, were limited. Most of the soldiers were quite young, only in their late teens or early twenties, like Khanh. But the women veterans in the collective were older, and the soldiers would have to address them as "big sister" or "auntie," according to tradition. That method of greeting inevitably built up a wall between the two groups that no one was daring enough to break through.

One Sunday morning, Nha woke up early, combed her hair, and carefully put on her makeup. Dissatisfied with her own things, she borrowed a red silk blouse from her friend Hien, and a necklace made of tiny seashells from Luyen. All of her co-workers gathered around her, helping her dress and make up her face, reassuring her of her beauty, and when she finally left, she was cheerful and pleased with herself. That was how the other women would remember her. None of them knew then that she had departed forever. By the next day at noon, she still hadn't returned. Everyone began to worry, but all the women could think of different reasons why Nha might be late. Then another day passed and they began to get angry and nervous. When she hadn't returned by the next Sunday, the women were frantic. They received word from the regiment that Khanh had waited all that last Sunday in vain. Had she gotten lost in the jungle? An emergency alert was issued. The regiment scouts and the women from the state forestry enterprise scoured the whole western section of the island. One day, another, three days passed. Nothing. The search went on in force for another two weeks, and for another month after that smaller groups continued to look for Nha. Although there were no predators in that primitive jungle, the trees and underbrush were so tangled and thick that some places had never been imprinted with the press of human steps. The jungle had swallowed any trace of the missing girl.

For some time after Nha's disappearance, no one, not even the bravest young women, dared to trek across the jungle from Viet Hoa to the collective's headquarters.

Time passed and fear faded. One afternoon, Hien gathered her courage and walked alone to the regiment base camp, to see her boyfriend. An hour later, crossing the road that led to Red Fish Lake, she felt a breeze blowing through the jungle canopy above her head and felt suddenly dizzy.

She sat down for a while to come back to herself, and then bravely continued her journey. Soon, however, she felt a strange sensation, as if someone were trying to lead her the wrong way. The field of wild grass that she knew marked the beginning of the trail had disappeared. Panicking, Hien retraced her footsteps and realized she had just missed the trail. A chill seized her. Just a second more, and she would have repeated Nha's bad luck. Like Nha, she came from the lowlands and was not skilled at navigating the jungle. Nevertheless, she had found the right way again and was determined to continue. Suddenly a flock of birds swarmed up around her, and from their chaotic tumble she heard a low, sorrowful call: "Nha, oh Nha, Nha!"

Terrified, Hien rushed back in the direction of Viet Hoa. As she did, she prayed: "Oh, Nha, you were wise when you were alive, and you have become sacred in your death. Please don't cause me any harm. Please bless me. We had no quarrels between us or hatred for each other. The day you left, you were wearing my red silk blouse . . ." Hien ran, the wind whistling by her ears, the trees swaying back and forth drunkenly. And the ghostly voices of the birds chased after her, crying clearly now: "Doom! Oh doom, doom!"

After that, no other woman walked alone through the jungle. Nha's disappearance and Hien's frightful experience hung like a gray shroud over the whole collective. Whenever they had to go to headquarters to work or to attend a meeting or even to see a film, the women only ventured out in groups. Their fear reinforced the feeling that the jungle had closed around them, surrounding them, keeping away any chance at love or happiness. At night they woke from uneasy sleep with the choked feeling of being hemmed in, cut off from the rest of humanity. They would hear the ghostly, agonized sounds of the birds crying from the jungle and a chill would pass through them.

The state forestry enterprise had been founded in 1976, a year after the American War. In 1982, a festive mood had swept the entire area when it was learned that the Cat Bac region was going to be designated as a national park. Once that occurred, the collective was placed under the management of the Board of National Parks. During the inaugural celebrations that marked the event, the women of Brigade Five had dressed in their best clothing and gone off gaily to headquarters so they could participate in the celebrations. On the last evening, they watched a film, then lit their torches and started back to Viet Hoa. But as they were making their way through the jungle, they were again struck suddenly by their solitude. They hugged each other and sobbed. With the establishment of the national park, their island was now officially a "forbidden place."* A forbidden jungle. How coldly that phrase echoed in their blood. From this day on, it would be illegal for anyone to hunt or take timber from the Cat Bac jungle. While this decree was good for the environment, it served only to isolate them even more. Forbidden jungle! But now they would be separated and forbidden themselves. Even before, this place had already

*Once designated as a national park, a region is protected from further development and population increase, hence a "forbidden place."

felt cold and lonely; now this seemingly innocuous change made them feel imprisoned, like nuns in a sealed monastery.

The situation lasted another year, until the day Luyen brought back news which cheered everyone up. One morning, along with Cuong the storage keeper, Luyen went to headquarters to get more farming tools and work clothes, as well as some crabs or fish they would use to supplement their poor meals. They flagged down a truck going to Cat Bac town. While she was there, Luyen stopped off to visit a friend at the export company and received some news that she eagerly relayed to the other women when she got back. "There's a new guy at Yellow Cow Bay. Someone from the city. I hear he's really good-looking."

"Did he take Phuc's place at the turtle rearing farm?"

"Right," Luyen said, then added thoughtfully, "But isn't it more correct to call it a turtle seeding camp?" She meant turtle breeding. The other women laughed. One said:

"Phuc is so afraid of his wife he doesn't even dare to put his own seed into her, let alone into the turtles!"

"Stop it—don't talk such nonsense. Listen, here's the best part." Luyen lowered her voice. "They say the new guy left the city because of a broken heart. But I hear he can draw so well his pictures look as if he'd taken a photo of someone," she added.

"He must be very talented," another woman murmured dreamily.

"Is there a way we can get over to Yellow Cow so we can ask him to draw for us?" a younger woman said, naively revealing her intentions. All the women burst into laughter, then hugged each other, still laughing, trying to hide their shame as if the young man had appeared in their midst. Yet even though they felt ashamed, each of them burned to meet the new man.

It seemed an impossible task. Yellow Cow was a small islet that lay in the bay to the east of Cat Bac Island. It would take only twenty minutes to get there by boat, but the eastern shore of Cat Bac consisted of a sheer cliff that was nearly impassable. The only way to get to Yellow Cow was to walk or hitchhike to the headquarters of the collective, then go by car to Cat Bac town and then continue by boat to Yellow Cow. None of the women had ever made that complicated journey.

Now the temptation and the frustration were agonizing. It took barely twenty minutes for them to get to the edge of that eastern cliff and look down at the cow-shaped islet with its grassed hills that turned yellow in the autumn. They knew that on that islet was a valley, and in it was an experimental turtle breeding camp, and at that camp now was a man; young, handsome, artistic, and new. They would go, some of the women, to the edge of that cliff and they would stand and stare and dream of the fulfillment of their hidden desire. Sometimes they had to fight back their tears. Even if they could climb down to the beach below, there was no boat for them to row across Yellow Cow Bay. He was so close, within reach of their gaze, but they could never meet him.

❧

The more the women of Brigade Five were being stirred like an ant nest before the monsoon by the arrival of this man, the more Mrs. Cay, Cuong's mother, let out her anger on Tham, her daughter-in-law.

"Fruitless tree! Childless woman! You're ruining the future of my family," she shrieked directly into Tham's ear. "This state forestry enterprise is overrun with unmarried women, all of them dying for a husband. My son could have as many wives as he wants. What a pity he had to end up with a good-for-nothing slut like you!"

She had harangued Tham with this cruel barrage for over a year. Tham feigned indifference, acted as though she had heard nothing. But the more she tried not to hear, the more clearly her mother-in-law's bitter diatribe rang in her ears. The words scratched at her brain and pierced her heart like thorns. Being single and childless was sad and humiliating; it was true. But being married without having children was even more so. It seemed as though happiness had eluded everyone in Brigade Five.

TWO

Tuong was the new man at the turtle breeding station. His journey to that place had been a long and strange one.

After finishing secondary school and passing the entrance examination to the Fine Arts College, Tuong had matured into a handsome man, tall, with an attractive oval face and eyes like a dove's, framed by long lashes. A friend of his, who took pride in his ability to interpret people's looks, once told him: "I'm afraid a man with liquid, shadowy eyes like yours will be immersed in unhappiness."

Tuong was not surprised at his friend's words. He had been orphaned when he was still a teenager: his father killed in action in Cambodia in 1978, his mother dead of a brain hemorrhage two years before that. He had been left alone in a tiny room on the second floor of a decaying building. But he refused to move in with any of his relatives—he had enough money to support himself from his student scholarship and his parents' insurance money.

He had first met Chi at a classmate's birthday party. In the midst of that raucous, bragging group, each striving to prove he was more artistic than the other, Chi and the friend she brought with her stood out—they seemed sincere, decent, and kind. After she'd learned that Tuong was an art student, Chi asked him to draw some pictures she could use as teaching aids for her class. As he listened to her speaking about her work as a teacher, Tuong found his interest piqued. The very next day, just as he had started to draw pictures for her, she came to his house with a roll of paper.

Tuong threw himself heart and soul into that work, and Chi happily brought the results to her class, inviting the artist along as her special guest. He stood next to the window and watched her with the children. He was delighted when she held up each of his drawings, one by one:

"What is this, children?"

"The tramway, teacher."

"And this one?"

"A tiger, teacher," they'd answer excitedly.

Tuong drew picture after picture for Chi and her students. He fashioned collages, made colorful posters, and used cardboard boxes to create puppet shows based on traditional tales. For weeks, he stood silently at Chi's window, watching his work being eagerly received by the students. He and Chi became more and more passionate about the project, and before long they began to feel the same way about each other. Soon they felt as if their lives centered only on each other and Chi's students, felt as if they were the only inhabitants of their own universe.

Then one day, her face distressed, Chi came to Tuong and said: "Someone told my mother about us. She's furious. She threw a fit and told me I was too young to be in love, and that you didn't come from a good background. She told me never to see you again, ever."

Tuong was devastated. He had been so caught up in passion and rapture that he simply couldn't imagine anything going wrong between himself and Chi. Now the world had caught up with them. Whoever betrayed them to Chi's mother must have squealed at some length: she knew both of his status as an orphan and that he was an itinerant artist with no other job, hardly someone who could provide Chi with a stable and happy family life. Hell, he thought, that must have been what worried her mother, not that nonsense that her daughter "was too young to be in love."

Chi's mother was a trader in cosmetics who ran a large distribution warehouse in downtown Hanoi. She had another man in mind for her daughter: Loc, a commissioner who worked as a middleman between the traders and the shopkeepers. She was very fond of Loc. He wasn't so handsome, but words poured out of his mouth sweet and neat as a dance. More importantly, he really knew how to kiss up to the shopkeepers. He was always ready to waste hours gossiping about what was happening in the neighborhood—from the fight between two jealous women, to the bitter and tawdry love affair between a fifty-year-old professor and his twenty-year-old student, to the fatal accident near the guardrail over the railroad tracks. Moreover, he was just as ready to spend money on theater tickets. In the late afternoon, he would help Chi's mother close and lock up the warehouse, then would hire a cyclo to take them to Dai Nam theater to watch "Miss Sita," or the cai luong* "Once I Was in Love" or to the movies to see the sentimental film "Love and Tears." Watching Chi's mother take out her handkerchief and wipe her eyes, then discreetly blow her nose, always made Loc happy. It was worth the price of the tickets.

Chi's mother sang Loc's praises to Chi as often as she could: "Loc is so smart, so hard working, so generous. Anyone who married him would be happy for her whole life! He has a Honda Cub motor scooter, a Sharp VCR and color TV, and so many other things he hasn't even taken them out of their boxes yet. What a wonderful young man!"

Chi was well aware both of Loc's generosity and his cunning. Once he had come to her house smiling hugely and bearing a large plastic gift bag in one hand and a bouquet of flowers in the other. He handed her the bag solemnly, then whisked around the room looking for a vase in which to deposit the flowers.

"What is this, Loc?" Chi had asked, wide-eyed.

"I wish for you the best of luck in becoming a year older, and I wish for you and your family good luck in your business and the continuous making of profits so you can enrich yourselves the more."

Chi was amused at his manner of speaking, and surprised at his words. "Who told you that today was my birthday?"

"Why, Mama of course." Loc put the flowers down and ran into the other room, calling out loudly: "Mama, didn't you tell

*A traditional performance: the wording here has the connotation of "soap opera."

me that today was our Chi's birthday?"

Chi's mother was busy noting down all her expenditures and profits in a small notebook. She pretended to scold Loc, her voice just loud enough so that Chi could overhear.

"What a man! You didn't listen properly. What I told you was that Chi was in her twenties, still in the prettiest bloom of her youth. And from that you took it that today was her birthday! Does that mean you'll bring her presents like this every day?"

Loc, right on cue, showed his embarrassment by shaking his head forlornly. He was so sincere and honest; he had just made a mistake. Would the ladies please not be angry with him? Oh of course not, dear boy, Chi's mother simpered. You're just enthusiastic because you hold so much affection for Chi, isn't that it? As Chi listened to this dialogue, she felt both amused and pleased. Loc was ridiculous, but he was a sweet talker and he knew how to please people. When he talked to the cosmetic traders, he became the tough negotiator, but he knew how to turn on the charm with her. Who didn't like to be praised, to hear sweet compliments spoken in a soft, smooth voice? She nervously opened the bag. Her face lit up as she pulled out an adorable light yellow Hong Kong Sport T-shirt and a pair of Adidas sneakers—she'd been longing for these things, ever since she'd joined the badminton club. She thanked Loc and accepted the presents graciously—but also somewhat impersonally. The result wasn't what he had expected. From then on, while she did feel affection for him, it was the emotion one would have for a brother. Often, she would casually refuse his invitations to the theater. Why not? She hated the sentimental operas anyway, and she didn't have to pretend with a brother, did she?

It was under these circumstances that Chi met Tuong and fell in love with him immediately, as if she had been waiting for him all her life. They were both passionate about art, about teaching, and about each other. And as soon as her mother found out about them, she immediately forbade their relationship.

"Listen," she shrieked, "I will not allow you to fall in love with anyone right now. And if you keep going with that orphan, you'll drive me out of my mind and I'll marry you off to the first fool I find!"

Chi was afraid. Her mother could very well carry out her threat. But if she obeyed, she wouldn't be able to see Tuong anymore. Her mind raced. Finally she thought of a way to calm her mother down.

"It's Loc you'd force me to marry, isn't it?" she asked maliciously, knowing this would distract her mother from the subject of Tuong.

Her ploy worked, at least for the moment.

"Do you think he's that easy to get? Dozens of girls want him, but all he cares about is you."

Chi had discovered her mother's weak point. If Chi showed any affection for Loc, her mother would purr, but if anything reminded her of Chi's relationship with Tuong, she'd go crazy. For weeks she scolded, ranted, and raved, finally telling her daughter she would commit suicide if Chi wouldn't break up with that man who "had attracted her with his witchcraft." Chi and her mother had reached an impasse.

One afternoon, Chi waited for Tuong in front of the Fine Arts College. She was worried, but there was a cunning sparkle in her eyes.

"It seems we've raised a fox in our chicken coop, Tuong. I found out today that it was Xuyen who told my mother about us. Listen, this evening I'm going to ask her to come to your place," she said slyly.

At dusk, Tuong waited anxiously for Chi in front of his house. Thinking of the cunning sparkle in her eyes, he felt a vague foreboding. Van, his downstairs neighbor, came out and teased him about his nervousness. She told him to go wait in his room; she'd bring Chi upstairs for him, instead of him hovering around here. Tuong was startled that even this young girl knew about him and Chi. How had they never noticed that so many eyes were watching them?

Chi and Xuyen arrived at a little past eight. Tuong reached out quickly to grasp Chi's hand. "Why didn't you come earlier?"

She stared at him coldly and slowly drew back her hand.

"I'm very busy, Tuong; from now on, please don't come to see me at my school anymore. I don't like it. You need to realize there are no special feelings between us."

Xuyen stared at her, shocked, while Tuong visibly stiffened.

"So, goodbye then, Tuong," Chi said. "Xuyen, don't we have tickets for the 8:30 show?"

Chi turned and left without looking back. Tuong leaned dejectedly against the door frame. The scene had unfolded just as Chi had planned, but to him it had seemed almost real. Perhaps that was why his heart ached now with anger and sadness. As he watched Chi's shadow being erased by the harsh light of the street lamps as she moved away from him, he felt that vague sense of foreboding again, and he feared that their love would come to a sad ending.

Two days later, Chi, laughing merrily, came to meet him.

"Everything's fine. This morning, Xuyen told my mother all about the other night. My mother feels great now."

From that day, Chi cut Xuyen out of her life without explanation. They avoided all the streets on which they might meet her, and they avoided other people who might know Chi. They would meet only at Tuong's or at the front gate of the Fine Arts College. But it was impossible to avoid everybody. One afternoon, they went to the August Cinema to see a new film. Suddenly a group of teenage girls on bicycles overtook them. As they passed, Tuong could hear their voices trailing behind:

"Miss Chi really is pretty."

"Van was right—she's beautiful."

"But a little thin."

Tuong was amused to see his little downstairs neighbor Van pedaling along with this flock of high-school girls. They must have followed him and Chi for a long time, just to check out his girlfriend.

❧

Once when they were together at Tuong's house, Chi said to him: "I don't like you hanging out with those so-called artist friends of yours. They're nothing but a bunch of phonies—all they do is drink and gossip."

Tuong lost his temper. "Look, don't criticize my friends. No one's perfect."

The confrontation turned into a serious quarrel that led to Tuong angrily storming out of the house. As soon as he'd slammed the door, Chi grabbed her things and left as well. But they could only stand to be separated for two days. Finally, Chi swallowed her pride and came to meet Tuong at his college.

That reconciliation, however, did not change her feelings about his friends, and Tuong remained angry at what he saw as Chi's intolerance. He thought that his friends were great. They were creative people: artists, musicians, film makers. Being with them was sometimes inspiring, and sometimes just a hell of a lot of fun. After one glass of wine they could build palaces taller than skyscrapers—they had ideas, imagination . . .

But although he didn't realize it, Tuong was the only true artist among them, the only one with a good heart. Chi was right—his friends were braggarts. The ones who called themselves painters drank and boasted more than they painted. The musicians were no better. Khang, for one, could only play a few chords on a guitar. He used his rudimentary knowledge to compose banal advertising ditties, then would slink into the offices of various businesses and factories and try to convince the management to buy his songs. He finally succeeded in selling one to a department store: *We sell what you do need or might / You're like family in our sight / We sell soaps and matches that light / And our clothes fit just right . . .* Later, he had another hit for a textile factory: *I grow the mulberry tree / and work in the textile factory / I help make our homeland beautiful / for the colors of our fabrics/are like the colorful flowers of our homeland . . .*

A typical night: While the group sat around drinking, Khang would relate his song-writing adventures, then clear his throat importantly and begin to sing, his tenor voice cracking and choking as if his throat were clogged with mucus. Meanwhile, Phung would talk excitedly about the films he had made in Haiphong and Hue. He always described himself as an "assistant director" even though he was really only a part-time contract worker for a film studio. If someone happened to mention the name of a young woman during the course of the conversation, Phung would declare bluntly that he had slept with her, and gleefully tell the group about secret points on her body, as evidence of his sexual prowess. His vulgar stories would weave into the eloquent voice of Du, "the barrel," an actor who always played minor roles in the theater, including one as a "walking barrel" which had given him his nickname. Despite these credentials, whenever Du opened his mouth quotes from Shakespeare, Molière, Brecht, and Stanislavsky would pour out like water from a faucet that couldn't be turned off.

An outsider, stumbling into this crowd, might get the impression he had come among a circle of great artists, men who shared the talents and weaknesses that all great artists supposedly had. Actually they were corrupt sneaks who called themselves artists or writers or musicians so they could extract commissions and state grants, and cover up their various con games and rackets. They talked constantly about "the arts" and saw themselves as creative people in order to give themselves an excuse to live in what they considered a bohemian atmosphere.

To make up for their lack of talent, they dressed the way they thought artists were supposed to dress, striving carefully to look carelessly disheveled and filthy, exaggerating the personality faults and quirks they believed marked artists. But the real artists felt tainted by their behavior and had to struggle to overcome the stink the group left in other people's nostrils. They spoke of Tuong's friends as a heap of foul rags, a stagnant pile of garbage that someone had forgotten to clean up.

Yet Tuong didn't see them in this light. He was dead serious about his own work as an artist. But he also thought it wasn't so bad to be able to hang out with a bunch of guys who could give you a few laughs and a chance to relax. And besides—though this was a reason he seldom admitted to himself—he wasn't brave enough to try to associate with more well-known artists.

Then one evening the police arrested him. When he arrived at the jail, Tuong was shocked to find the whole gang there: Khang "the musician," Du "the barrel," Phung "the assistant director" and so on . . . as if, he thought, they'd decided in unison to make this cell their new gathering place. They'd been stripped of their artistic clothes, and of their cockiness and sophistication also. They acted like old jail birds. They fought, cursed, snatched up each others' rations as well as the necessities their relatives sent them. Soon, listening to snatches of conversation that surfaced during their endless quarrels, Tuong began to piece together what had happened. A long time ago, his friends had put together a scam organizing phony boat escapes for people who wanted to get out of the country.

They'd managed to swindle their clients out of a good deal of property and money, so anxious were their naive victims to seek a life abroad. That scheme was the only true "masterpiece" that Tuong's friends had ever created.

Tuong was kept in jail for a month while the case was investigated. Finally, he was found innocent of all the charges and released. But in the meantime he had been expelled from the Fine Arts College.

Much later, when he had calmed down, Tuong could see how the people who expelled him had good reasons. But for the moment he was stunned and confused. His head was hot and pounding, as if hundreds of jackhammers were beating incessantly inside his skull, smoke rising from their bits. He wanted to punch down the doors of the college officials and demand that they change their decision. When the rage finally left him, he felt exhausted and torn, as if all the joints of his bones had been pulled apart. Would he have to stop painting, kill the passion that had moved him since his early childhood . . . the images and lines and colors that he loved more than anything in his life?

Well, he still had his beloved, didn't he? The whole month he was in jail, he longed for Chi to visit, just once. But she never came. He strove to find excuses for her. It was difficult for a teacher to have a relationship with a criminal. Moreover, her mother was always watching her—how could she get away? Anyway, it would have been terrible for Chi to come to the prison, sit awkwardly across the table from him, see his skinny body covered with mange, his hair shaved in the prisoner's style.

But even after she knew he had been released, she hadn't come to see him.

Didn't she realize he could never be involved in such a scheme? Did she think he was the same as his thieving friends?

But maybe, he thought, she did believe in his innocence, but was mad at him for hanging out with those "artists." Maybe his arrest was the last drop in her already full glass of suffering.

He was suffering himself. Days of pain and desperation, anger and fear. Finally, he could stand it no longer. One evening, he mustered the courage to go to Chi's house. He climbed up to the window of her room, the way he had secretly come to meet her in the past. She wasn't there. Well, he'd already burned his boats, so he figured he had no choice but to enter by way of the front door, in a more dignified manner. As he did, he saw Chi's mother, busy inspecting some cosmetic kits from France, Japan, and Hong Kong that had just been delivered to her by some retailers. A banal love song was blasting out from the cassette recorder on the table near her.

"Good evening, ma'am," Tuong greeted her properly, no longer feeling the nervousness he used to whenever he saw her.

Perhaps the music from the cassette recorder was too loud. It was not until the line: *Oh, it's over—I wonder if you know I have been longing for you loneliness,* was finished and he had greeted her for the second time that Chi's mother looked up and took notice of him.

"Oh, it's you." She moved the cosmetics to one side and grinned at him. "Please sit down. Sorry I'm busy with these things. Won't you have some tea?"

Tuong was astonished at her cheerful mood. Maybe she hadn't recognized him. After all, he'd only met her once or twice. Maybe she thought he was one of her customers. He didn't want her to continue under a misperception, so he asked bluntly:

"Ma'am, is Chi here?"

"Why don't you just sit and relax and wait for her, Tuong? She'll be back soon." She spoke with the smug confidence of a general certain of imminent victory. "Loc took her out early this afternoon. They're very busy deciding what they'll need for their life together. Anyway, it's good for Chi to get married this year. Twenty-two is an auspicious age, you know. It's so complicated, isn't it, Tuong—getting married? As the saying goes, one has to consider the wife's age to get married, the husband's age to build the house, and so on."

He hoped she couldn't see his face go pale in the dim blue light of the neon lamp. He refused to show his emotions in front of this woman who would be only too happy to watch him collapse. A male singer whined from the cassette recorder: *Oh nothing remains, nothing remains but sorrow . . .*

Tuong strove to keep his voice calm. "Is everything good with your business?" he asked.

"Thank you for asking. In fact, it is—something I owe, I'm sure, to my being so pleased with Chi's happiness."

Again the whiney voice from the recorder: *There remains nothing to dream, to long or hope for . . .*

He wanted to smash the damn machine. But he maintained his poise. After what seemed like a decent interval, he stood and said politely: "Well, I just wanted to drop by and see you and Chi. But it's getting late, so I'll have to say goodbye now."

He sensed her victorious eyes on him and tried to walk out with his head up, his eyes straight ahead. It was only after he'd turned onto another street and was sure no one was watching him that he let himself stagger, his hands trembling. He nearly fell against a Volga parked at the side of the road.

That night, he went to a cafe near his house and drank a glass of whiskey. He was hungry and had nothing to snack on and no friends to commiserate with. Soon he slumped onto the table. Later a cold drizzle blew into the empty cafe and he felt a chill and woke up and paid for his drink and started home. He staggered along the road to his house, then squatted over the sewage drain and vomited uncontrollably.

"My God, brother Tuong: what happened to you?" a voice said in his ear.

He vaguely recognized the image of a young girl hovering above him. She tugged at his memory, but he couldn't place her. She helped him to his feet and brought him into the house and laid him on the bed and washed his face with a cool, wet towel and it was only then that he recognized Van, his young neighbor from downstairs, through the haze in front of his eyes. He forced a weak smile. He felt guilty and ashamed in front of this young girl.

"Thank you, Van. But please go home now."

After a few days, he forgot everything that had happened that day and that night. Only a few blurry images remained, like the remnants of a dream. He didn't believe what Chi's mother had said to him. He smiled as he remembered the days he'd stood by the window in Chi's classroom. "What's this? . . . That's a car, teacher . . ." Their love was pure, without calculation or malice. How could Loc's shadow fall over it? No, clearly Chi's mother had lied. She'd always wanted to destroy her daughter's love for him. He had to meet Chi again, find out what had really happened.

Once again he found himself clinging to her window ledge. He swung himself up smoothly and was about to drop in. Then he froze and almost fell.

The curtain was pushed to one side, blocking the view from the upper half of the bed. The two naked people lying there wouldn't be able to see him peering in. Nor could he see their faces. But he could see Chi's legs, beautiful as a Venus in white marble. He could see them being caressed by a chubby hand that grew from a short, fat arm. He could see the two fat legs on top of them, entwining around them—Loc's legs clinging to Chi's.

He felt paralyzed. But his mind was cold and clear. He would do nothing else, would ask no more questions. Those four entwined legs were the answers to all his questions. The complete affirmation. There was nothing else to find out. He remembered Chi's cunning expression on the day she'd schemed to trick Xuyen. Inside her existed both the innocent and the wicked. Perhaps his passion for her had prevented him from seeing Chi's true nature.

Again, he tried to drown himself in whiskey. He wanted to forget it all. He couldn't. Drunk, he saw himself floating through the clouds. "What's this, children?"

"It's an airplane, teacher."

"And what's this?"

"That's an arm, teacher."

"And what's this?"

"That's a leg, teacher." A leg. A leg. A leg. A leg.

One afternoon Xuyen knocked on his door. Without waiting for him to open it, she pushed inside, her face frightened.

"Tuong!" She pulled him up from the bed, shaking his shoulders, which were loose as a bag of meat. "Tuong, Chi is dead . . ."

"Dead?" he mumbled, trying to open his eyes. "That's nice . . ."

Xuyen cried, her voice choking, "Tuong, didn't you hear me? Chi is dead. She was hit by a truck."

Tuong sat up and stared at her, the consciousness of what she'd said flooding his mind. His eyes reddened. He nodded to let her know he understood.

"Loc took her shopping for their wedding party, yesterday evening," Xuyen said, seeing Tuong's eyes registering comprehension. "A truck hit them as they were coming home, along Hai Ba Trung Street. Chi's skull was crushed and she died at once. Loc is bruised all over and one of his legs is broken."

A leg. Again a leg.

Tuong went to Chi's house that afternoon, for the funeral, even though he hadn't been invited. It had rained a few days before and the road was still muddy. Chi's mother screamed and sobbed horribly and tried to break away from the arms of the women holding onto her tightly. Tradition forbade her from looking at her daughter's face for a last time before the coffin was closed, nor was she allowed to follow the hearse. It rolled slowly down the muddy road, bumping over the potholes filled with dirty water. The music played by the funeral orchestra sounded eerily like whines and sobs. People queued silently behind the car and followed it down the narrow road in a solemn procession. Suddenly a truck appeared, coming from the opposite direction and heading straight towards the people. According to custom, all mistakes made by the dead person are forgiven. Thus the truck—that reminder of how Chi died—should have pulled over and let the funeral procession pass. Instead it moved stubbornly forward, forcing people to leap to one side. As the truck passed, the driver gunned the engine loudly, spewing black smoke on the mourners as he roared past. His wheels bounced through the puddles, splashing mud onto the hearse and the line of people standing behind it.

"My God, how inhuman he is!"

"He must be crazy!"

"Stop him! Stop him!"

Tuong was splashed as well. The muddy water dripped down his face. He wiped it away. The angry voices echoing around him drove him mad. The truck almost got away, but it had to slow down as the road became narrower. Tuong ran to it, threw open the door, jumped into the cab, and punched the driver in the face. Maddened, he pulled the man out, threw him down onto the muddy road and continued to pound his face mercilessly. He punched and punched, feeling he was punching into Loc and Chi's flesh . . .

The other mourners quickly leapt in and pulled him off. A traffic policeman walked up and sternly ordered both of them to go to the police station. Panting and puffing, Tuong walked past the hearse. He was aggrieved to see the white funeral wreaths attached to the side of the car covered now with black mud. The two white wreaths became the two white legs of Venus . . . and the chubby hand that caressed them. Wherever the hand touched, the white skin turned black and greasy, as if being painted with mud. But soon the white wreaths covered with mud blurred and faded from his sight. He covered his face with both hands and sobbed.

Tuong and the truck driver were locked up in a cell inside the police station for the night. It wasn't the same cell he'd been in before. The police discovered that the truck driver had been drunk, and cut off one corner of his license.

"I'll tell you, my fate's nonstop up and down," he confided to Tuong, as if the two of them had never been in a fight. "First I get my old license confiscated by the cops, then I take a new test to get this one—now it's almost completely cut up. This afternoon, I get a job hauling sand for twice my usual rate. I was happy as hell, and then I ran into that damned funeral . . ."

Suddenly a policeman opened the door and pushed in a girl dressed in thin clothes, her face caked with makeup. The smell of cheap perfume emanated in waves from her body and filled the cell.

"Hey, honey." The truck driver slit his eyes and leered at her. "How'd a smart Hanoi whore like you let yourself get caught on the streets?"

"When you need money, you walk the streets; don't matter if you're a Hanoi girl or a 'machine' from the sticks," the girl said bluntly, sitting down next to the driver. Hearing her hoarse voice, Tuong thought she sounded familiar. He turned around and stared at her.

"Is that you, Len?" he finally asked.

Shocked, the girl looked at him. "Oh God, Tuong. I was so dazed I didn't recognize you."

Len was the daughter of some people who owned a noodle soup shop. Her family, Tuong knew, was well-to-do: the Len he knew had never had to work to make a living. Most of the time she'd hung around with one group or another, looking for different ways to amuse herself. She'd modeled nude for the art students, without asking for money, and had even brought poor students to have pork soup at her father and mother's shop. She not only took off her clothes for these would-be painters, letting them contemplate and make practice sketches of her body, but had also fallen in love with one of them. Their passionate affair had lasted for two years, until the day the young man graduated and married a deputy minister's daughter. Len had just laughed bitterly, but from then on she refused to model for any more painters. She vowed to herself that nothing and nobody would ever hurt her again. She would never fall in love again with any filthy man. From then on, she threw herself into gambling, drinking whiskey as if it were water, smoking like a factory chimney. At times, when she was completely disgusted and disillusioned, she also took to wandering the streets at night, playing the role of a prostitute.

"So why are you here?" she asked Tuong. "I remember you used to be a very serious guy."

The driver put his arm around her and pulled her away from Tuong. "Hey, sweetie, don't waste your energy on him—he needs a rest after the fight I gave him. Come on over here with me, honey."

Len wriggled away and pushed her elbow into his chest. "Get your stinking hands off me, you disgusting beast."

She came and sat down next to Tuong. Suddenly she grabbed his face in both her hands and drew him to her lips as if she were drinking from a coconut. Her lips clung to his. The white wreath, covered with mud, whirled around in Tuong's mind. This girl was sunk in foulness, covered by it. He pushed her away, suddenly terrified, but she threw herself on him again, frantically, like a thirsty vampire. Why not? part of him thought. Who was he being loyal to—Chi?

As he grasped Len and pulled her to him, he saw again the four naked legs behind the curtain. Len began to lie down, drawing him with her. He released his grip and let her fall to the floor. What was he doing—she was probably filthy with disease . . .

He was brought early the next morning to the police station office. A policeman wrote down his name and address, briefly scolded him, and let him go.

❧

When he woke up, the sky outside his window was just starting to darken and the shadows had lengthened in his room. He sat up and started to reach for some water, then remembered he hadn't boiled any for days. As he let his head drop back on the pillow, he saw a shadow beside his bookcase.

"Who's there?" he asked, startled.

The shadow rose, flowed to the edge of his bed. He saw a cascade of long hair, dreamily watched the shadow form into a young girl.

"It's me—Xuyen," she identified herself. "How are you feeling?"

"I'm OK, just a little tired."

Xuyen looked around for the switch, then flicked on the light. Seeing her in it, Tuong realized for the first time what grace she had in her face. When she saw some life had returned to his eyes, she sat down happily next to him.

"I just met with a former classmate of yours—Huy. He said he wanted to get together with you, plan a way you can force them to take you back into the college."

Tuong waved the idea away. "Don't be so naive— there's no way I can go back. Don't talk about it."

Xuyen sat down beside him. Exhausted, Tuong closed his eyes and began to doze off again. He felt a hand shaking his shoulders, Xuyen's voice echoing in his ears.

"Tuong, you need to get up, have some noodles. You haven't eaten all day."

She took his meal container and went out. When she returned, she brought a large bowl of *pho* to his bed. Suddenly realizing how thirsty and starving he was, he brought it to his lips and devoured it. The warmth of the food made him feel stronger, more relaxed. He leaned his head back against the wall and breathed in deeply, watching Xuyen as she washed the bowl in the corridor. When she returned, he smiled at her. "Tell me, Xuyen—why did you go to Chi's mother about our affair?"

Xuyen calmly dried her hands and sat down next to him.

"First of all, Chi's family was obsessed with money and possessions—they weren't at all suitable for you." She spoke slowly and precisely, as if carefully considering each word. "Secondly, Chi was a very impulsive girl, but she was also very fickle and could be swayed easily by material things, or by a sweet voice."

He saw Chi standing in front of her students, holding up his pictures: the car, the train, the station, the elephant, the bear, the rabbit, the turtle . . . he saw her lips moving without a sound coming from them, as in a silent film. He got out of bed, went over to the tea table, and poured himself a cup of rice wine from the half-full bottle.

"I haven't finished what I want to say," Xuyen continued. "Thirdly, Tuong, you were out of your head then; you didn't really understand what Chi was. She contained many contradictions, that girl. She was an innocent, but at the same time, she knew how to keep things from you that she didn't want you to know. The whole time she was dating you, she was going out with Loc to parties and festivals."

He remembered the night Chi had broken up with him, in front of this woman. He had sensed something of Chi's slyness then, and now Xuyen had confirmed his suspicions. Better to forgive and forget the errors of the dead. But the bitterness remained in his heart, and he wondered if fate had taken a kind of twisted revenge on Chi for him. No, he didn't want to think that.

Xuyen went on, oblivious to his deep reverie, determined to say everything that had been on her mind.

"During the days following your arrest, Chi's mother and Loc hovered around her constantly. Loc poured presents into her hands; he kept distracting her with gifts, inviting her to come with him for picnics at Tam Dao and Dai Lai. Her mother kept nagging at her too, telling her how you'd said you loved her, but really planned to escape abroad and leave her behind and had never told her. She said you had a police record now and had been expelled from the college, and would have a hard time finding work, with no family, no property, no profession—how could Chi give up her future for you?"

Tuong gulped down the rest of the wine and climbed back in bed. He found himself staring at the swell of Xuyen's breasts under her blouse.

"That was really why Chi changed her mind," she said.

He suddenly felt dizzy and leaned his head back against the wall again, looking up at the ceiling. "What about the fourth reason," he said.

"What do you mean, the fourth reason?"

"I'm not that drunk yet, Xuyen. Tell me the truth—was it only for those three reasons that you went to Chi's mother and tried to destroy our love?"

Xuyen shuddered slightly. She bent her head and sat silently for a moment, then looked up at him.

"You're right. I did it because I loved you too."

Tuong shot forward like an eagle and grabbed Xuyen. Shocked, she tried to struggle against him. But by now, Tuong didn't know what love was. All he could see was the four white legs framed by the curtain. He wanted only to break, to cut, to stab. To smash them.

❧

In the days after this incident, Tuong for the most part stayed home. Now and then he went out to a bar and drank rice wine. He wanted to stay drunk forever. But he couldn't. He wanted to sleep forever. But he couldn't do that either: the loudspeaker from the district cultural house across the street kept blaring announcements into his room. Over and over the announcer kept bleating about the New Economic Zone being created in Lam Dong Province. Tuong covered his ears with his hands and turned his face to the wall. His need for sex, so long dormant, began to torment him again. Sometimes when he was with Chi, working on a painting, she would sit next to him, lean her body into his. He had wanted to throw down his brush, hug her, caress her, take her—but he'd always controlled himself, resisted. He'd wanted to preserve his love, remain pure until their marriage, all of that crap. Now, frustrated and angry, he let himself go. What was there to preserve anymore? Had Chi preserved anything? He wanted to get back at her, at Loc, at all those miserable, so-called artists. At Xuyen too. He'd seduced her with his lies about love. After that night, she hadn't dared to come back. Maybe she was still frightened of his horrible strength.

He had finally hit bottom. No more money for whiskey. Not a grain of rice left. Without bothering to even figure out what they were worth, he brought his American jeans to the black market. A mob of traders rushed over and swirled around him, eager, pushy, jabbering at him. They passed the jeans around, offering one price, then lowering it when they saw he didn't react. In the blink of an eye Tuong found himself standing alone in the middle of the sidewalk without his jeans. Inside a nearby tea shop, a group of young men looked at him and burst into laughter at this stupid hick who'd just been cheated. Tuong stood, nearly crazy with anger, on the verge of tears.

That same afternoon his cousin dropped by. Seeing Tuong's desperate situation, he went back home and brought Tuong some rice, then invited Tuong to stay with his family. Tuong refused. He couldn't bear to be near anyone right now. He didn't want anyone to see him falling apart. He had nothing left. No family, no friends, no girlfriend. Why should he continue to live? Since he had stopped studying art, he felt uninspired to start anything else. When he walked down the street, he felt hundreds of eyes were looking at him, their stares piercing his skin like arrows. Look, there's the fool whose girlfriend cheated on him, then dumped him. Look, there's the guy who was thrown in jail and expelled from college. He was afraid of being known, afraid of being alone. When he'd first become an art student, he'd had an oil painting displayed in the Municipal Exhibition Hall, and used to drop by now and again to see if anyone would stop in front of his painting and comment on it. Now he was afraid of comments. He was sure that everywhere he went, people were gossiping behind his back, starting all sorts of rumors about him.

He wanted only to avoid everyone. Lying on his bed, eyes closed, he touched the night stand and then began to grope for his sleeping pills. When he'd been a student, he'd had trouble sleeping and had gone to the college's clinic to request some medication. Once he received it though, he just left it by his bed—he'd been afraid of the side effects from Western medicine that he'd heard about. Now he poured all the pills from the bottle into his palm—there were about a dozen. Then he shook out all his tetracycline and penicillin tablets. High doses of antibiotics were poison too. Without hesitating, he swallowed all the pills in a few quick mouthfuls, and then crawled into his bed.

First he felt like vomiting. A moment later, the muscles in his belly quivered, then his whole body began to tremble and twitch, as if it were being turned inside out. *What is this, children? It's a ship, teacher. And this? Teacher, it's a coffin.* The stiff legs . . . white, spread-eagled wide, as people tried to force them together . . . the grave full of water, the dead person's relatives must have forgotten to pay off the grave diggers . . . the coffin carelessly dropped in the hole, dirty water splashes, freezing water. Tuong panicked, struggled up, staggered to the stairs. The faded and broken steps rolled under his feet like waves. He nearly fell, but some instinct to survive allowed him to keep his balance, stagger to the door of the apartment downstairs. It was slightly open. He could dimly make out a figure, a young girl sitting at her desk.

"Van . . . oh Van," he called out.

"Brother Tuong, what's the matter?" Van dropped her pen and rushed to him.

He clamped one hand on her shoulder and held onto the doorknob with the other to keep from falling.

"I've taken . . . sleeping . . . pills."

"My God." Van pushed him down onto the bed. "Stay here; I'll call a cyclo."

A few minutes later she was back with an old cyclo driver. The two got Tuong into the cyclo and carted him to the hospital.

❧

Van was waiting outside with her bicycle on the day he was discharged. Her father had wanted to come with her, but she had demurred. "Daddy, he's terribly ashamed of himself and would be embarrassed if many people came to see him."

Finally, Mr. Chinh had agreed with her and let her go alone. On their way home, Tuong drove and Van sat on the back of the bicycle. She leaned over and told him to head to the August Cinema.

"I got the tickets this morning," she said. "I figured we could go directly from the hospital. You know, Tuong, when my cousin Hoa was home, I only went out to the movies with him."

Her sweet sincere voice was full of laughter, but it also held a slightly wheedling tone that usually made everyone obey her wishes.

He'd shared a house with Van and her family for a while

now: they were on the first floor, Tuong on the second. But until recently he had barely spoken to her. He'd always considered her a little girl, and every now and then would tease her when he came downstairs to get water from their shared tank, or when he stood outside, waiting for his friends. As for Van's father, Tuong respected him but hesitated to talk to him. Mr. Chinh's dignity intimidated him. He'd never heard Chinh raise his voice. He seemed to live a harmonious, stable existence, marked by love and respect for everyone.

Van's mention of the movie tickets spurred his memory. At times, when Tuong had been very busy or had just forgotten to go to the market, he'd turn Van into his "logistical assistant," and ask her to go buy vegetables and fish for him, or wash his vegetables and rice. She'd agree immediately, but always ask him for compensation. "What kind of compensation?" Tuong had asked the first time. "A ticket to the cinema, brother Tuong. But only if you'll come, and come by yourself. I won't sit with your 'artistic' friends. Not Chi either—all she'll do is sit and glare at me." Tuong suddenly understood what was beneath Van's teasing—she was an only child, without a brother to take her to the movies or the opera. He recalled how she would tell her classmates to follow him and Chi, how they would giggle when they passed by, Van's voice drifting back to him, calling out, "There's my brother Tuong."

The film she brought him to now was called *Sport Lottery '82*. Tuong's mind was burdened with many things, but still he found himself bursting into laughter several times during the movie. But the predictable happy ending, complete with the reunion of the lovers, made him feel vulnerable. As the credits rolled, he felt himself reverting into the gloomy and silent personage he'd been when he left the hospital. He knew he'd return home in a few minutes, back to the stares and gossip of his neighbors. And, in fact, as soon as he braked his bicycle in front of his house, Tuong caught a group of women staring at him as they squatted on the pavement buying guavas. He ignored their stares, lowered his head, and pushed his bicycle into the vestibule. Human beings! Why must they watch every single move of other people? Why did they have to gossip, draw legs onto the image of a snake, even invent stories about other people. If that was how people showed their "concern" for others, how on earth could people live peacefully under that burden? Now, besides all the other sobriquets heaped on him, Tuong would have a new one: the failed suicide. The realization horrified him.

That evening he had dinner with Van's family. Mr. Chinh put some fried fish into Tuong's bowl.

"You know, I wanted to advise you to choose better friends," he said, "but I never really had an opportunity to speak with you before. Now it's too late. It's nice to have good intentions, but if one acts on them too late, it's worse than being indifferent, isn't it?"

Tuong looked at him in surprise. He'd always assumed Mr. Chinh had faulted him for all that had happened. Yet it seemed that Chinh blamed himself.

"Enough, daddy . . ." Van glanced quickly at her father, willing him not to remind Tuong of the past.

"No, please go on." Tuong shook his head slightly at Van. He wanted to hear what her father had to say.

"It may be too early for me to ask you this, since you haven't had time to think about it . . . but I'd like to know what you're planning to do now."

"Uncle." Tuong put his bowl down and looked straight into Mr. Chinh's eyes. "I decided what I'd do while I was in the hospital."

"Are you going back to the Fine Arts College?"

"No. First, I don't think they want me back. More importantly, even if they did, I'm not brave enough to face my classmates and suffer their gossip."

Since his attempted suicide and his subsequent recovery, Tuong had felt his spirit revive somewhat. But living in his old flat, facing his neighbors in the street, making a few minor changes, then going back to his old way of life? No. Just thinking of it made him shudder. If he continued to live that way, he'd just be wasting his life.

"Then what do you intend to do?" Chinh asked, an undercurrent of concern in his voice.

"I want to find a place where no one knows who I am, what I've done, where I've been. I want to rebuild my life from nothing."

Mr. Chinh, his wife, and Van waited in silence for Tuong to continue.

"I've thought about it very carefully. The government is encouraging people to go to the New Economic Zone. I'm going to volunteer to be sent to Lam Dong."

The silence continued for another moment. The only sound was the cat scratching the leg of the dining room table and mewing for more food. No one said, "Ah," in approval; no one seemed shocked; no one protested. Mr. Chinh seemed to be deep in thought, caressing his freshly shaven chin with his thumb. Finally, he said: "If you've considered this carefully, then I have nothing to say. But I would like to suggest another possibility. If you want to get far away from here, then what about Cat Bac Island? You could try living there for awhile, and if you didn't like it, you could come back."

Van clapped her hands in approval. "He can go to cousin Hoa's place, is that it?"

Her father nodded. "I have a nephew who directs the Cat Bac Export Company. I'm told he's very progressive, and doesn't judge people for their family history or past problems. Whoever is willing to work hard and faithfully is welcomed by him."

Tuong imagined Mr. Chinh as an artist, slowly drawing out a scene for his eyes: a lush island in the archipelagoes of the northeastern coast. In the middle of that landscape, so attractive to landscape artists, appeared the idealized figure of the young director painted by Chinh's words.

Mr. Chinh grew more excited as he told Tuong about his nephew. "Maybe you already know him? When your family first moved here, Hoa had just graduated from the Economic Planning College and was assigned to Cat Bac Island."

Van was even more enthusiastic. "It's been almost nine years now, daddy. I don't think brother Tuong knew Hoa then." She turned to him. "But you might remember that time two years ago when cousin Hoa came here for his annual leave and used to take me to my after-school courses?"

Tuong nodded. He remembered a tall, slim young man,

though he couldn't picture his face. At the time, he would not have imagined his life might be so closely linked to Van's family, to this man, Hoa.

That night, back in his room, Tuong considered his choices. For the most part, all he wanted was to get away, which both options provided. But the idea of Cat Bac Island seemed more attractive to him.

The morning he left, Mr. Chinh gave him a letter to Hoa, relating Tuong's story and asking his nephew to help him. As his bus left Nua station, Tuong looked back at Van until even her shadow disappeared. Until now, all the old familiar streets had bored him, but as he was leaving, he realized how much he would miss them. He thought of the young girl who had taken him to the bus station, her solitary shadow remaining on the pavement. Van, he said to himself, Now you're the anchor steadying my boat; the string that holds my kite as it soars further and higher . . .

THREE

Tuong would have died of loneliness if Phuc hadn't been with him during his first days at the experimental turtle breeding station.

When he first started working at the company's offices in Cat Bac town, he had heard all kinds of gossip about Phuc and his wife, most of it concerning the way she constantly henpecked and threatened her husband.

Once, a story went, Phuc had been complaining to his friends about her fierce temper when she'd unexpectedly walked in on them. Phuc had paled and, turning to his friends, hurriedly whispered, "Oh God, she's here. Only say good things about her so she won't harm anyone." Another time, Phuc had been seen fleeing his house and sneaking away through a maze of streets, his wife in hot pursuit. When she caught him, she forced him to put on an old cotton jacket so full of holes it looked as if it had been riddled by bullets. At his wife's insistence, Phuc had worn that jacket every day for ten years, but that morning he had simply become too ashamed to put it on anymore and had tried to sneak off to work without it.

Such stories about Phuc's poor, henpecked personality were numerous, but Tuong refused to believe them all. He was too familiar with the way people gossiped. Still, on his first day at the station, when he rowed over to the beach to say hello, Phuc's first words were: "Did my wife tell you when she'd row over here to take me home?"

So the rumors about this couple weren't total inventions. Though they had met several times before at the company offices, Tuong looked at Phuc as if seeing him for the first time, then laughed and said: "You're lucky. I left early this morning and didn't see her."

"Just wait," Phuc grumbled. "A few days from now, she'll rush over here and drag me home."

He and Tuong had walked up the narrow sand beach to a three-room thatched house. Inside were two bamboo beds, some chairs, and a desk which functioned also as a tea table. Several wooden boxes were stacked in a corner of the main room.

"What's that—our food supply?" Tuong joked.

"Incubators for the turtles—part of the breeding experiment we're conducting now. But the results haven't been good. Many of the turtles hatched in them were weak and deformed, some with missing legs, their heads twisted or their backs bent, so they died prematurely. I told the director from the beginning that no incubator would work as well as natural sand."

Tuong walked back to the front door and looked down into the open concrete tanks that housed the healthy turtles. Phuc followed him. In contrast to the gloomy mood he had always seemed to be in when Tuong had first met him, he seemed cheerful, as if relishing Tuong's company after being alone for so long on the island.

"We maintain ideal conditions in these tanks: the turtles are reared in sea water and fed regularly."

Tuong stood there for a long while, watching turtles of various sizes and ages milling about. The baby turtles swam on the surface, using their rear flippers like oars, while the older turtles lay silently at the bottom. Golden drops of sunlight flickered over the blue water, reflecting off the flowery patterns on the turtles' shells.

"These other tanks," Phuc explained, "are used to monitor the effects of changes in the turtles' diets. The water has the same degree of salinity, but the turtles aren't fed as much. In the next tank, they're fed regularly, but the water is fresh. The ones you see here are about a year old and have lived in fresh water for over a hundred days already. You can find the data in the notebook on the desk."

Tuong glanced at the slope behind the house. The wind whistled through the myrtle trees.

"It's very sad being here, isn't it?"

Phuc's face darkened. His left hand skimmed the surface of the water in the tank next to him, gently splashing the turtles swimming languidly in the center.

"Actually more lonely than sad." He straightened up, shaking his hands dry as he walked out to the beach. "I sometimes think that living in a crowded city is much sadder than living somewhere else in solitude. But that's just my opinion. It may very well be sad here for you, since you're still so young."

"Well, since I asked Mr. Hoa to let me be your replacement, I guess I can bear it."

Despite his bravado, Tuong knew it would be hard to be alone here. It would be sad. Nevertheless, he pictured himself getting used to the solitude and the silence. He would bring his oils and acrylics and easel to the beach, like the classic impressionist painters. He would capture on canvas the sudden, fleeting changes in the myriad of colors he saw everywhere in this place, the subtleties of sky and sea, of dawn and dusk. What would it matter if he wasn't acknowledged by the academics or the critics or the galleries? He would be an Henri Rousseau, a Van Gogh, even if only for his own satisfaction.

The next morning, Phuc had rowed him around the smaller islets near Yellow Cow, stopping at the various places where female turtles nested and laid their eggs. At one point, he brushed aside the sand and showed Tuong the eggs.

"When they incubate naturally like this, a higher percentage of turtles actually hatch and there are fewer deformities. But the eggs are always threatened by something . . . being eaten by monitor lizards, or even being drowned in a heavy rain." He paused. "Do you think you'll be able to remember all these different sites? You're responsible for watching all of them."

He covered the eggs again, then shook his head. "Don't worry. When these are about to hatch, I'll come back and help you check on them. It'll take some time for you to get used to the job."

Tuong offered him a cigarette, then turned his back against the wind as he struck a match. Both of them sat down cross-legged and smoked silently.

"Were you born here?" Tuong asked.

"No." Phuc's face darkened slightly. "I used to live in the city."

Tuong remained silent, thinking Phuc would continue with his history. But Phuc just closed his eyes and inhaled deeply, holding the smoke inside his lungs for a long time, his chest puffed with the effort. He exhaled slowly.

"A little while ago I discovered a hidden beach, where the big turtles come to nest." It was obvious Phuc didn't want to discuss his personal life. "Since the tides are high this month, we'll wait until evening, then go there and catch a mother turtle."

Despite this innocent talk about turtles, Tuong saw that Phuc looked strained and nervous. He knew something bad must have happened to Phuc. But in a few more days, Phuc would go back to Cat Bac town and Tuong might never hear his story.

That evening, they rowed out to a small island deep inside the bay. A perimeter of rocks sheltered the wide, flat beach from the wind. They hid behind one of the larger rocks. Phuc stared at the sand.

"I'm from the city, just two hours from here by motorboat, and yet here I am where it takes me two hours by motorboat to get to work. I didn't know a thing about turtles until the day I enlisted during the American War. I was assigned to the special underwater forces, and trained in Cat Bac town. When I was sent to perform my missions, in the south part of central Vietnam, I was 'adopted' by a turtle hunter in Phan Thiet, and lived with him as his son. I learned about turtles from him."

"Is he still alive?"

"He died in 1974. He helped us sink enemy boats for years, without getting a scratch. But just before liberation, he was killed when some traitor informed on him to the enemy."

Phuc leaned his head back against the large rock, sinking into memory. The wind blew strongly from the sea. The relentless waves bit into the beach.

Eventually, Phuc sat up and shook his head, as if to clear away the old memories.

"OK, now you tell me—why would a talented and handsome young Hanoian come to this island?" he asked Tuong.

"I have my reasons."

Director Hoa, Van's cousin, was the only person at the company who knew the details of Tuong's story. He knew the stories of everyone at the company, all their intrigues and secrets. But he told no one and, as Mr. Chinh had promised, refused to judge his workers on their pasts, only on how well they did their jobs.

"Apparently we both have some history we can't speak of," Phuc said, sighing.

Tuong took a deep breath, trying to stave off his sudden gloominess. He changed the subject.

"Are there any good-looking girls around here?"

"You won't even see a man's shadow on the sand for days,"

Phuc muttered. "Why would you expect to find any women?" But then he suddenly pointed to Cat Bac Island to the west and the formidable cliff that rose in front of them. "You want to meet some women? Right over there, boy—Brigade Five, all of them single women. Go right ahead."

Like inviting a person to sit on a hot stove, Tuong thought. The idea was tempting, but also a challenge. Who could scale that rocky wall? Probably the only way to get there would be to take a boat around to the other side of Cat Bac, nearly a day's journey itself, and then trek for another day through the jungle and over the pass to the women's encampment.

The two men remained silent for a time.

Around eleven o'clock, just as Tuong's drooping eyelids were about to close, Phuc poked him sharply in the ribs. His eyes shot open. Something with the shape of a large bamboo tray was moving ponderously and carefully up the beach. He watched, squinting, as the female turtle stopped at an area where the sand was flat and solid and slowly began digging out a nest with her flippers, making a swimming motion against the sand. Tuong had never seen a turtle this big: the diameter of its shell must have been eighty centimeters. When she'd finished digging and scratching out a hole, the turtle nestled herself into it, her face towards the rock perimeter, her tail pointing to the sea. She began laying her eggs.

Tuong watched wide-eyed. A light breeze caressed his face soothingly. Normally, it would make him feel sleepy—but instead he was wide awake, on edge. The turtle was only about five paces from them. Why didn't Phuc move? Maybe he was waiting for the turtle to finish laying her eggs. But what a long time to wait.

Phuc slapped his side lightly, signaling him to remain still. Then he rose into a crouch and glided silently around the rocks, flanking the turtle. She had finished laying the eggs and was covering them. Laboriously, she slid her body forward, flattening and smoothing the sand over the eggs. Then she edged slowly back towards the line of surf, her face still to the rock perimeter and her tail to the sea.

Phuc leapt from behind the rock, still moving lightly and silently. The turtle raised her head and began scrambling towards the water. Phuc rushed after her. Seeing him, the turtle turned around and scrambled away faster. Phuc chased her. When he drew parallel, he stooped down and chopped into her neck with the side of his right hand. The turtle halted, stunned by Phuc's blow. Phuc stretched his arms across her shell, grasped under its edges, and strained backwards, lifting the turtle towards him. Finally, with one fierce jerk, he stumbled back and the turtle flipped over onto its shell. Her little flippers waved wildly in the air.

Tuong jumped up excitedly and ran over to Phuc. He grabbed his hand and pumped it. "Congratulations!"

Embarrassed, Phuc pulled free. He turned his face to the side to hide a satisfied smile.

"What a goose you are. Go over to the boat and bring back the rope and shoulder harness."

Once they'd secured the turtle, the two men gasped and grunted as they carried it back to the boat. When they'd returned to their camp, Phuc split a bamboo pole and built a fire in the sand. Then he sat down next to the turtle. The firelight reflected off the netted drops of sweat on his shoulders and chest. At that moment, there seemed no trace of the city dweller left in Phuc; he was truly a fisherman.

"Tomorrow I'll bring this turtle back to the factory and give it to Hoa personally."

Tuong grinned. "Aren't you afraid people will say you're kissing up to him?"

Phuc rolled his eyes as if Tuong had made exactly that suggestion. "This isn't a matter of a relationship between director and subordinate. This is brotherhood. If I like someone, I'll show my feelings; I don't care who or what he is."

After a few moments of awkward silence, he said: "You have a tongue just like a gossip's."

Tuong laughed. "I just wanted to remind you how people are. You know I like Hoa as much as you do."

Phuc had been right about his wife. Early the next morning, just as he was about to leave, Mrs. Nu appeared, rowing a boat, ready to bring him home. For over a year, she'd been complaining constantly, demanding that her husband be transferred back to headquarters in town. She had a harsh personality, a way of speaking that made people feel she was scolding them, even when she felt sympathetic towards them.

"Whose company have you been enjoying so much you haven't had time to make it home yet?" she yelled to her husband as soon as her boat was beached.

Phuc pointed to the turtle inside his boat. "Hers."

Nu glanced at it. "Is that for Hoa?"

"Why not—everything is for Hoa!" Phuc glared fiercely at his wife, but couldn't maintain the pretense of anger and almost immediately burst into laughter. "Great minds think alike, my dear—you had the same idea I did."

"Shut up, great mind!" Nu scowled menacingly at her husband, then changed her tone. "Early this morning, as he was walking me to the harbor, Hoa asked: 'So are you finally satisfied that your husband will be at home?' I just shrugged and said 'That's how it should be. My family was like a troop of beggars when we first came here, and you helped us, gave us jobs and a home. Reassigning my husband to headquarters is just a small thing for you to do. But I'm not fully pleased with you—that will only happen when you finally get married. If you agree, I'll give you my younger sister, for free.'"

The couple bickered loudly as they packed Phuc's things. It wasn't until they were about to row away, that they remembered Tuong, standing and watching them.

"When you come to town, be sure to drop by our house, Tuong," Nu shouted as they rowed away. "I'll make you some noodles and bamboo shoots."

Tuong watched them until their boat disappeared behind an islet.

❧

When he had been in the town, working in the company office, a co-worker in the company had taught Tuong how to cast fishing nets. Now, every morning, he rowed out the boat Phuc had left for him, and positioned his nets. The small fish he caught were used to feed the turtles in the tanks, while the larger ones—flying fish and red fish—were for his own meals. He prepared fried fish, boiled fish, and sometimes fish soup. He was getting sick and tired of fish.

Worse than the monotony of his diet was the solitude. The experimental turtle farm had once belonged to the aquatic products factory. Later, Hoa had launched a campaign to produce the turtles directly for export, making it necessary to establish a breeding station. His idea was accepted by the district leaders. Besides the section in charge of purchasing chameleons, prawns, crabs, and squids, as well as oranges, lychees, and forestry products, Hoa also began raising goats and buying products from local fishermen. The turtle breeding station was just part of his plans to enlarge the export company's operations. Phuc had been assigned to the farm when it was first established, in order to get the experience necessary to make it a fully-functioning operation. After sufficient trial and error, testing, and development, Hoa planned to expand the area of operation. For about a year now, however, Phuc's wife had been nagging him constantly to bring her husband back. Nu was normally very jealous anyway, and couldn't let Phuc out of her sight for a day. Now he was away constantly. How could she trust a man with his characteristics? Tuong had heard about the situation after he'd come to Cat Bac, and after thinking about it for a while, decided to ask Hoa to be assigned to the turtle breeding station. Hoa seemed to have too many things on his mind, and Tuong thought his offer would at least relieve this small headache.

He had expected the loneliness. And it had been months now since his difficulties in the city. But still he felt restless and empty, as if he were constantly missing out on something. He had wanted to come to a no-man's land, to escape to a place where no one knew him. But he was used to being a part of something, of a city and a country where one lived one's life entangled warmly and constantly with other lives. In that was both suffering and meaning. Now he felt too cut off. Each day, besides taking his measurements, setting up his schedule, noting data in his record book, Tuong tried to create his own joy by sitting down with his easel and paints. When he was painting, he forgot everything. But soon darkness would come. By dusk, the waves would lap monotonously at the sand, encroach on the beach until they nearly reached the turtle tanks. Tuong would sigh, light the big kerosene lamp and start reading. But where would he find enough books to read every night? Sometimes, gloomily, he would simply turn off the lamp and go to bed early.

It was then that the secret instincts and lusts he'd tried to hide away began to revive, to stir inside him. He tossed and turned on his mat. The bamboo bed creaked and groaned under his body. He saw four legs wrapping around each other, rubbing slowly against each other. He saw Xuyen's body in the grasp of his own fierce desire. When thinking of women, he often saw them in these positions. To his horror and self-disgust, he realized he was starting to picture Van in the same way.

❧

In the morning, after setting out two of his nets, Tuong decided to row further out into the bay instead of going back to the farm. Ahead of him were some boats collecting the saliva of dolphins to sell to pharmaceutical companies. The boats moved slowly, searching for the dolphins. Soon Tuong saw a dark blue area expanding on the light blue surface of the water. It couldn't be the shadow of a cloud: the sky was spotless. Immediately, an old fisherman, his sinewy arms corded with veins, pushed a bamboo pole into the thick blueness. As he pulled it up, Tuong saw a thick, glue-like liquid dripping from it.

The men in the boats cheered.

He rowed past them. He was facing the western slope of Cat Bac Island now, looking up at the sheer rock wall, thickly overgrown with bushes and vines. There must be some way up it, but had anyone ever dared? He wondered if the women of Brigade Five were somewhere over the top of that cliff. Was nature's separation and prohibition of human beings from their sexual needs any less severe than that imposed by human beings on themselves?

As he rowed closer, he saw that at the foot of the western cliff was a beach, facing the bay but walled from it by an island, creating a calm harbor. He'd thought Phuc had shown him all the beaches where the turtles laid their eggs—but why not this one? It was so large and flat there had to be at least one nest. Suddenly pleased with his discovery, Tuong rowed to shore.

He imagined it would take all morning to investigate the beach. If Phuc hadn't brought him here, perhaps it was because it really wasn't a suitable nesting area. He studied the sand carefully, looking at all the small trails and traces for the telltale signs of an egg nest. A crab scuttled by, dragging its little seashell house. Some gulls cawed shrilly as they floated above the beach, searching for prey. Tired and a little frustrated, Tuong flopped down on the sand. He realized that since setting foot on this beach, he hadn't stopped thinking about the women in Brigade Five. He didn't know who they were, or what they did, but he could picture them going to and fro, chatting to each other as they worked. He squinted against the harsh sunlight, peering up the rocky slope. It looked like it might be climbable. But was it really? Perhaps it was simply that no one had ever dared try?

Suddenly, as if in answer to his questions, he saw someone climbing down the cliff. When the person was closer, he saw it was a girl, dressed in dark blue worker's clothing. As he watched, she grasped the limb of a tree and swung down, her feet searching for a hold. In that way, moving from branch to rock, she continued to descend.

That same morning Luyen had broken away from her comrades and their job of extracting *huong nhu* so she could come to the edge of the cliff and gaze at Yellow Cow Island. It was a habit she had fallen into lately, and although she never saw anything in particular, somehow the act made her feel secretly pleased and somehow comforted. She suspected that the other girls would also sometimes wander over here to stare expectantly at the smaller island. Who or what they waited for was difficult to say. The longing that seized them was so vague and in many ways so unfamiliar as well. But today was different. Not long after she had come to stand at the edge of the cliff, she saw someone row a boat into the bay, then pull up onto the beach. No one had ever been seen on that beach before. The unexpected visitor wore jeans and a striped shirt, and although she couldn't see his face clearly, something in the way he moved made her sure he was a city person. He walked slowly up the beach, a tall young man searching for something in the sand.

He looked so close that Luyen had the feeling she could magically swing over the rocks and land at his side. How bold I am, she thought, laughing at herself, but at the same time feeling a heat coursing through her entire body. It somehow focused her, made her purposeful and strong, and when she looked down at the rocky cliff, it no longer seemed so formidable to her. She knew, if she remained calm and moved with skill, she could make it to the beach: it wasn't that far down from where she stood. What worried her more, what made her anxious, was the thought that the man would soon leave. Forcing herself to keep her mind clear, she began to descend.

Tuong was also nervous at the prospect of meeting this stranger. He walked hesitantly over the rocks towards her.

"Good morning," Luyen said shyly. "Do you work at the 'insemination farm'?" She caught herself and blushed. "Sorry—

I meant the turtle farm."

Tuong hadn't noticed her embarrassment. "I've just been assigned there. Are you with Brigade Five?"

It was his turn to blush. He was ashamed of that person hidden inside himself, his desires and fantasies about the women in Brigade Five.

Neither of them knew what to say now. They had each recognized and acknowledged what they wanted; they had each sensed the other's desires boiling inside their own bodies. But it was too simple, too quick, to start like this. Where could they go from here?

Tuong stepped forward clumsily and took Luyen's hands in his own. She turned quickly towards the bay, drawing his eyes after her stare, making him wonder if she'd seen someone watching them. But he saw only the gulls, hopping on the sand or circling through the air, searching for fish or shrimp.

"When I was climbing down the cliff," Luyen said finally, "I saw the opening to a small cave." She drew her hands back, embarrassed, realizing the naked intention of her words. She continued, haltingly, trying to hide her shame. "It looked very beautiful. Would you . . . want to have a look?"

Without waiting for him to answer, Luyen turned her back to him, walked to the cliff, grabbed the edge of a rock and swung herself up. Tuong scrambled after her. One moved ahead, the other followed. One was above, the other below. Each wanted to turn this quiet game of hide-and-seek into the romantic chase of lovers. But they had only known each other for a few minutes. How could they talk about love? So it was that each fantasized they were playing a love game, but they kept their fantasies to themselves.

There was indeed a cave, and as Luyen peered inside, she saw it had a flat floor and was truly quite beautiful. On her way down, she had just glanced inside, but now she had the chance to look at it carefully. Just beyond the opening, a row of stalactites hung like a white curtain. Tuong, coming up next to Luyen, felt a sudden shock: the shape reminded him of the curtain to Chi's bedroom, the way it hung to one side. He felt a fire burning inside him; in front of his eyes, he saw a vague image of Chi's face. He reached out and grasped Luyen to him and hungrily pushed her to the ground, brushing aside her initial shy cries of refusal.

It was eerily quiet, with only the sound of the wind whistling outside the cave.

"Oh," Luyen said. She picked up a piece of bamboo near the place they were lying, and showed it to Tuong. "Someone has been here? But who else would climb to this place?"

Tuong sat up and took the bamboo from her hand. The section was as long as his arm, and one end had been burnt, with ash still stuck to it. Her question echoed in his mind: who else could have come here?

"Let's go in and have a look."

"No, no, I'm frightened," Luyen whispered.

Her fear excited him. He put the bamboo down and smashed its burnt end with a small rock, then lit a cigarette and held it to the feathered edge until it caught fire. Holding the torch in front of him, he led her into the cave.

It was very cool inside. The walls around them were beaded with moisture, as if they were sweating. Bats appeared and then disappeared into the darkness beyond.

"Oh God!" Luyen clutched his arm tightly.

Just beyond where the cave curved off in front of them was a white silhouette. Tuong stared at it, slowly realizing what it was: a stalagmite that looked remarkably like a naked, reclining Venus. His former classmates would be astonished if he brought it back to Hanoi.

He took two more steps—and then stopped with a shock as Luyen screamed and wrapped her arms around his waist from the back. There against the other side of the Venus stalagmite was a skeleton. Perhaps, while dying, that person had rested his or her head against the rock, leaving the skull where it was now. A tattered red blouse hung from the bones. Around the collar of the blouse was a seashell necklace.

Tuong stood numbly. He was aware of Luyen's breasts pressed against his back. Neither of them moved.

The flame of the torch was beginning to die. Tuong came back to himself, and quickly let the embers drop, then held the stick upside down to make the fire blaze again. Luyen started to loosen her grip. As he turned to help her out of the cave, she screamed suddenly, her voice horrified.

"Oh my God, it's Nha. And my seashell necklace . . ."

She rushed back to the cave's entrance. Tuong followed her, terrified, holding the torch high so she could see the way. Once outside, Luyen stood as motionless as a tree trunk, leaning her head against the rock wall of the cave, Tuong forgotten, the frightening, exhilarating game they had been playing forgotten. Her thoughts were focused on her poor friend. Maybe Nha had missed the road that day, wandered through the forest for days, then tried to climb down the cliff. Maybe she'd been overwhelmed with exhaustion, hunger, and thirst and had sought refuge in the cave.

Ignoring Tuong's nervous glances, Luyen climbed back up the mountain, following the same zigzagging, perilous path she'd descended only a little while before.

❧

Back at Brigade Five, she dashed by the processing workshop for *huong nhu* extract and rushed into the workers' quarters.

"Oh, sisters! Nha . . ."

Everyone threw down their work and surrounded Luyen. She was pale and breathless.

"Why did you mention Nha's name? Did her ghost come to haunt you?"

"What did you see, Luyen? Where?"

Luyen threw herself on her bed. She was exhausted, her hair a wild mess, and the questions of her colleagues came to her as a vague roar in her ears. After a while, she calmed down and began to explain how she had found the cave. "I saw Nha there," she said. "She died there . . . still wearing my seashell necklace."

Her calm explanation and her determined tone convinced the other women that what she was saying was true.

"We should bring her back to us," one said.

"Oh Nha, Nha, Khanh immediately took another woman as his wife. You poor girl," a middle-aged woman lamented.

Mrs. Mien, the head of the team, waved her hands. "Enough. Go get your tools, some plastic sheets, and some ropes to help us climb. Luyen, get up, wash your face, and then show us the way."

Everyone scurried to obey Mien. Soon, more than a dozen members of the team had gathered with their poles, axes, and ropes. As they walked across the big yard, Mrs. Cay, Tham's mother-in-law, ran angrily to the door of her house and shrieked at them:

"Tham, you get back over here!" She turned to her son, Cuong, who stood deferentially next to her. "You tell your wife to go home. It's the middle of the day—doesn't she have anything better to do than go traipsing off with the other women like that?"

Tham was furious, but she knew she had to obey her mother-in-law. She waved sadly at the others as they walked away.

Mr. Vien, the head of the processing section, was walking towards them. Mrs. Cay turned to him angrily.

"You and my son are the only two men here, but neither of you seem able to control these women? Aren't you the Party secretary?"

"Who can call us men?" Mr. Vien answered gloomily. "For a long time now, these women have seemed to think we're the same gender as they are. Sometimes I feel so ashamed at their jokes and behavior, I want to find a hole to hide myself in."

❧

The women stood without moving in front of the skeleton that had once been a lively, cheerful girl. Carefully, they gathered all the bones and wrapped them in a plastic sheet. Two women walked in front of the rest, the plastic hanging down heavily from the shoulder pole they bore between them. But at the mouth of the cave they stopped, unsure how they would be able to get her back up the cliff.

Mien took charge. "Use your poles to lever away those rocks," she ordered. "Whoever has a knife, clear brush for a path."

Another time, a different place, and the women would have protested against her ordering them around, but to her shock, everybody got to work immediately. It wasn't only because of Nha. Mien herself had at times wandered over, drawn, to stare down the cliff. Many times. The other women had had the same desire. Now, with the occasion of bringing home Nha's bones, they had a reason to open a road to the beach below. None of the others knew about Luyen's experience that morning, but deep inside themselves, they knew what having a path down to the beach meant. They knew the distance to "the other side" would be shortened.

A few days later, the path was completed. The women now had a little bit of hope.

FOUR

Two months before, Tuong had stood gazing curiously around the compound of the export company. It consisted of two two-storied blocks of flats, facing out from the flank of a mountain. Clothes lines were set in front of each door, and it was difficult to tell which room contained the company office. He finally decided on the rooms at the end of one of the buildings. Gathering his courage, he walked through the door.

The man inside seemed collapsed over his desk, his bare arms stiff, the muscles in them taut, his hands gripping a notebook. He was staring transfixed at the pages, muttering numbers and figures like a mad man. As Tuong's shadow fell on the book, he looked up with a wry expression and waved the notebook wildly.

"I understand nothing!" he shouted.

Tuong burst out laughing. He hadn't had the time to ask if he was in the right place, but his question had been answered anyway. The man stuck his nose back into the book and its jumble of data. At the desk next to his sat a woman, pecking rapidly at an Optima typewriter. To the other side of the entry door sat a young man with long hair and a fierce expression.

He was tapping his fingers nervously against his knees.

"Is this the company office?" Tuong asked him quietly.

The young man barely had time to nod before the older worker shouted again: "I tell you I understand nothing! This data is a mess! And everyone says it's so easy to be an accountant."

An accountant. Tuong could see he wasn't suited for the job, that he probably should have been doing some sort of manual labor. He leaned his easel against the wall, removed his knapsack and shoulder bag and placed them on the floor next to the easel, and sat down next to the young man.

"Is Mr. Hoa here?"

"I'm waiting for him too."

The secretary looked up from her typing. "There's green tea in the pot; please help yourself. Mr. Hoa should be back soon." She turned to the accountant. "Calm down and look over the numbers again. The more nervous you are, the more mistakes you'll make."

The accountant exploded. "Stop bringing me bad luck! When I'm like this, it's better just to leave me alone."

Tuong was intrigued by the strangeness of the man's features. His mouth and nose protruded forward, accentuating his receding chin. He looked like a seal. Since it seemed he had some time on his hands, Tuong took his notebook out of his bag and began to make a sketch. A seal's nose and mouth appeared, jutting forward provocatively, as if ready to attack. But the eyes were sunken, worried and frightened, seeking escape from the dreaded chaos of numbers. Energized by the work, Tuong replaced the accountant's hair with two seal's ears, then linked the head to a round, chubby back.

"That's very good!" The sound of laughter behind him made Tuong jump. He turned. A tall, slim man was grinning down at him. Tuong didn't know how long he'd been there.

But somehow he knew this had to be Hoa. Embarrassed, he started to close his notebook, but Hoa snatched it from him. He glanced impishly from the sketch to the accountant and back again. Finally, he looked at Tuong, his eyes twinkling. "Amazing similarity," he said. "Afraid of everyone, but still can't help provoking them all the time." He started to hand the notebook back, then hesitated and asked: "Is it all right if I keep this sketch?"

Before Tuong could answer, the other young man rose. "Mr. Hoa," he said, "my father told me to come and see you."

Hoa turned to him, registering surprise at first. Then a look of recognition broke over his face and he took the young man's hand warmly. "Is this Dai? Yes, I remember speaking to your father about you. Unfortunately, I have to leave in a few minutes for a meeting with the People's Committee. But I've heard so much about you already . . ."

"What have you heard?" Dai said nervously.

"Take it easy. Any mistake you made belongs to the past."

Hoa walked Dai to the door, and pointed to the entrance of a room on the ground floor of the apartment block behind the office.

"Tomorrow, you'll report to Mr. San, the head of Purchasing. He's arranged a job for you as a buying agent for forestry products. You'll have to travel out to the forestry station quite often. But at least there's a bus running out there now—the trip's much easier than it has been."

After he'd said goodbye to Dai, Hoa smiled at Tuong. "Are you a landscape artist? We've had several other painters visiting the island recently." He held up the notebook. "So—will you give me that sketch?"

Tuong took the notebook back, but instead of tearing out the page to give to Hoa, he opened the back cover and took out a letter.

"Mr. Hoa, this is a letter from Mr. Chinh and Van."

"Really?" Hoa reached for it eagerly, then motioned for Tuong to sit down as he opened the letter. "How is my uncle? And my little cousin Van—is she growing up too fast?"

He read the letters, smiling occasionally, his eyes sparkling.

At one point Tuong saw his smile vanish, and Hoa glanced down from the letter. Tuong felt his body go tense: he was sure Hoa was reading about him. But soon the sparkle returned to Hoa's eyes, and Tuong let himself relax.

Hoa folded the two notes and put them back in the envelope, staring intensely at it, as if he were looking at his two relatives themselves. For a minute he sat and smiled. Finally, he turned to Tuong, his eyes focusing on him as if he'd just realized he was there. He poured some tea and gestured for Tuong to join him.

"Have some tea, then go and put your things away in my room. You'll be my roommate—at least I won't have to be afraid of being lonely any more."

Suddenly the telephone rang. Hoa went over and picked up the receiver.

"Yes, this is Hoa. From where? The pharmaceutical company? What do you mean they weren't prepared correctly? You want to return all of them? Listen, five hundred chameleons aren't just a few lizards! What do you mean proper way? Dried, on cross-sticks? My God, there isn't a word about that in our contract!"

Hoa slammed down the phone and frowned. But when his eyes met Tuong's, he smiled again. "A lesson about not being too casual when drawing up a contract. What the hell am I going to do with five hundred chameleons?"

He bent down and picked up Tuong's knapsack, then escorted him to the room. It had two single beds, a desk, and a small cupboard. "Take whichever bed you want." Hoa pointed out of the window to the backyard. "If you'd like, you can wash up in the bathroom over there. I have to go pick up some chameleons."

As he walked out, he called: "Dan, can you help me out and go to the market for some food? I have a guest from the mainland."

After taking a bath and washing his clothes, Tuong returned to the room. Two large bags were propped up in one corner. Hoa and a young man Tuong hadn't seen before were standing in the center of the room. Both were sweating heavily.

"Tomorrow morning someone's going to have to take these chameleons to the city and sell them to get some of our money back," Hoa said, downing glass after glass of water.

"Who do you want to send?" the young man asked.

"Everyone's busy. Anyway, it's better to know some of the people in the offices where we can possibly sell them. I'll have to go myself."

Tuong looked dubiously at the two huge bags. "Alone?"

Hoa smiled. "Want to come along?" When Tuong nodded, he clapped his hands together. "Done. I'll borrow another bicycle for you."

When the other young man left, Hoa extended his hand. "I haven't forgotten. Let me see your sketch."

Tuong passed it to him. Hoa lifted the glass tabletop and placed it underneath. "From now on I can laugh whenever I look at Sang's face. I always wondered what kind of animal he resembled, what kind of animal would seem both very kind and very threatening at the same time. A seal—how perfect!" Hoa's expression turned serious and he lowered his voice. "I hope you can help me with the accounting. In a company that handles millions of dong it's not a simple task. Sang wants to return to the fishing boats—he's been asking me to send him back for a long time now."

By the end of their meeting, the director of the municipal vegetable and fruit company agreed to buy the two hundred chameleons. Tuong was surprised by Hoa's skill as a salesman. His own artistic talents contributed to the negotiations as well—he'd quickly drawn a sketch as a gift for the director.

"At times like this, I feel almost ashamed when I look at myself speaking the way I do," Hoa said as they bicycled through town. "But once you get involved in trading and purchasing, you realize that sometimes you're going to have to be pragmatic, sometimes mischievous, sometimes innocuous. I often have to do things which, deep inside, I don't want to do."

Hoa stopped and gazed down the street. Along the bank of the nearly dry river were several flower shops designed in the old way, with roofs of Chinese tile. Nearby a municipal theater displayed posters advertising new comedies. But Hoa's mind was still on business. "A friend of mine directs an export company in the Vinh Bang district. He became too casual in checking up on his employees, and didn't realize that some of his workers had spilled water onto a batch of drying lychees in order to increase their weight in the shipment. You can imagine what happened. Both the quality control inspector and customs investigated the company when they found out about the spoiled shipment. Everything was returned and the workers had to use brushes to clean each lychee and dry them a second time. Of course, then they were sold for a ridiculously low price. The company lost both time and money. The worst part was, it wasn't until the lychees had been shipped abroad that they received a telegram about the fungus that developed on them. They had to send people overseas to inspect and retrieve the goods and try to resell them at a greatly reduced price. That's how it goes. Just because the company neglected to do one small technical check, millions of dong were lost ..."

Late that evening, Tuong and Hoa ate dinner at a small restaurant. Afterwards they went to the home of an acquaintance of Hoa. The house only had two rooms, but their host cheerfully gave them one room, about ten square meters in size, and he and his whole family jammed into the other.

"It might be difficult for you to sleep," Hoa said, gesturing at the single bed they would need to share. He seemed to hesitate. Tuong was already lying down, his knees drawn up, since he was too tall for the small bed. He noticed Hoa's hesitation and pushed himself against the wall.

"Please take the outside," he said. "If I lie there, I'll just fall off anyway."

Hoa lay down, but kept his eyes wide open. His mind still seemed to be on business. He chattered away to the sleepy Tuong:

"For a whole year, what worried me most was not having enough goods to export. Not that importing was any easier. Once I was allowed to import 1000 meters of cotton cloth. For exactly the same type of cloth, you can charge customers 210 dong if it's blue and 180 if it's gray. But when you buy the cloth from the manufacturers, both colors are the same price. I had to nag and cajole this storage manager for a long time before he'd agree to sell me some blue cloth. The ink on the purchase order was barely dry when he asked me bluntly to give him enough cloth to make a shirt for him and a blouse for his wife—a payoff, you understand, for getting me the better-color cloth at a good price. If you were me, Tuong, what would you do? I wanted to punch the damn guy. But I controlled myself and thought about my uncle, Mr. Chinh. My uncle is very Zen—he's always calm, and he's always demonstrating to us, his younger relatives, how to be calm in the same way. So after we received the cloth, I took out a few meters and asked one of my staff to bring the material secretly to his house. I lost some meters, but each meter gained an extra thirty dong when we resold it, with a total profit of about 30,000 dong in all. That's how it goes. On one hand, we have to struggle against corruption, but on the other, we can't be too picky. I know, though, that many people condemn me for acting like that . . ."

Tuong said nothing. But his eyebrows were raised as he listened to Hoa speak to him, as if he, Tuong, were his younger brother. He knew Hoa was often held up as the new model of the young businessman. Yet even the most perfect model couldn't help getting a little dirty. The hell with it, he thought fervently. Was it better to be someone who sat back and criticized or looked for ways not to do something, or to be someone who did the work, even if it meant making mistakes and getting your hands dirty sometimes? If he had to choose, he'd choose the way of the businessperson, even if it meant being attacked by those who would cling to the old ways.

"Is your work your only joy?" he asked Hoa hesitantly.

Hoa chuckled. "Last year a newspaper reporter alleged the same thing in an article he did for the municipal paper. I don't accept it, nor should you, Tuong. I'm passionate about work, work, and more work . . . but it's not because I've forgotten myself. If I forgot myself and my other needs, I wouldn't be me anymore. I look at it this way—everyone has his passion, his goals, his desires. For me, the desire to prove myself, to show others I can work hard and be successful, has chased away all the other desires. I remember when I was thirteen or fourteen, I was assigned to be in charge of the children's organization on my block. Some of the older neighbors who didn't like kids would get angry when they ran and yelled and played outside, calling them 'good-for-nothings.' I arranged a meeting with the seniors' group, and encouraged the kids to help out the old people's families. In turn, they agreed to give the kids a dozen xa cu saplings which had been cultivated by the old men. One Sunday morning, I took all the children and we planted the trees along the street. Now they're thriving and beautiful, growing in front of our houses. It was just a matter of getting the old people to recognize the capacity for good that existed in the children. My current situation is the same. There are too many people in the district Party Committee and district People's Committee who don't believe in our abilities. They criticize me for taking the capitalist road, for running after profit. They accuse me of hiring staff with 'improper' or 'unclear' backgrounds—they've even accused me of hiring gangsters, and have demanded that the entire company be 'investigated.' Look, I know all about the rumors and allegations—but my business has brought a lot of money to the district, and since I've not done anything unethical, I feel this is the best way for me to prove myself. Proving I'm capable and better than my colleagues is a thing of joy, don't you think?"

Tuong rolled over and faced the wall. As he was drifting off, he suddenly remembered the young man he had met in the company office the day before.

"Who's Dai?" he asked.

"He's the son of someone on the staff of the Agro-Forestry Department. When he was in his early twenties, he went to prison for some time for assault and robbery. But I knew he'd changed considerably since his release, so I agreed to hire him. Having a steady job, in a well-managed organization helps a person stay honest . . ." Noticing Tuong shifting fitfully, he asked: "Will you have trouble sleeping in this narrow bed?"

"No, I'm fine. Sleep well."

When Tuong awoke at dawn, he found he was alone in the bed. Sitting up, he saw Hoa sleeping peacefully on some old newspapers he had spread out on the floor.

❧

After he had worked a month for Hoa, Tuong became the sign painter for the entire district capital.

It started when he asked Dai, who knew a bit about carpentry, to cut some small, thin boards for him. On them, using bright red paint, Tuong painted the name of each section of the company. Soon signs proclaiming *Information, Accountant*, and so on, marked the office doors. At the entrance to the block of flats was a larger sign stating: *Export Company Living Quarters.* Tuong had remembered the first day he'd come to the island and had stood at the crossroads, unsure which way to go to find the company. He'd finally had to ask someone directions. Now a big yellow sign with red letters, posted right at the crossroads, directed customers coming from the mainland. This simple act, he felt, made the company more attractive to both staff and customers. One day the secretary of the district People's Committee noticed the sign, and looked up Tuong at the company office.

"After working hours, could you please make some signs for our committee and the Party Committee? It encourages people to work better when they have an attractive working environment."

But Tuong's main job at the company in those days was as accountant, keeping the books and managing the company's records. The duties were not that arduous and he had plenty of time after work to paint his signs. Visitors to the island were amazed at the sudden blooming of signs and poster boards wherever they looked. Every fifty meters, on every electric pole, hung a sign or poster with red words on a yellow background. It looked like the town was permanently preparing for an important conference or festival. Soon everyone knew that a talented painter was working for Hoa's company. The locals, curiosity piqued, tried their best to find out about Tuong's background. But their efforts were in vain. The only person who knew Tuong's story was Hoa, and as was his custom, he refused to utter a word.

One morning Tuong found a small piece of wood, about fifteen by thirty centimeters. Soon a new sign would decorate the entrance of the room he shared with Hoa: *Bachelors.* Hoa came in while he was working on it, and smiled as he read it.

"Do you know if my cousin Van is still painting?' he asked suddenly. "She used to be quite good at it."

The remark surprised Tuong. He had never paid much attention to Van, except when he was teasing her or asking her for help. He'd never even thought to talk to her about her painting, even though she knew he was a student at the Fine Arts College. Oh Van, he thought, it's only now when I'm so far away from you that I begin to miss you, and want to take care of you . . .

Hoa's questions stirred so many memories in him. He saw

that Hoa had remained silent, just watching Tuong's brush as it glided across the board. His eyes seemed vacant, as if he were staring at nothing.

"I'm the youngest in a family of four children," he said eventually. "My father died when I was two years old, and my mother stayed a widow so she could take care of us. Her salary and what she earned for the work she did on the side as a seamstress weren't enough to make ends meet, let alone to send my brothers and sisters and I to school. As soon as I was old enough to start school, my uncle asked her to let me live with him and my aunt. She gave birth to Van seven years later. I loved my cousin very much. I'd take her with me to the movies or to soccer games. Once when I went to a match and only had one ticket, she insisted I take her along. Since two people couldn't get in on one ticket, we both went home instead. That's how it was with us. When I graduated from college and was assigned to Cat Bac Island, I hesitated at first. One reason was I couldn't imagine what I'd do in such an isolated place. But another was I didn't want to leave my cousin. She was only nine years old. Who would protect such a sweet and fragile person growing up in Hanoi? Every time I thought about her, my heart ached. And I wasn't wrong to worry so much. Two years ago, when I went home on leave, I had to walk her to her evening classes every night. Some parts of the street between her house and the school had no electricity and there was a gang that would hang around and harass the younger girls, and sometimes even rob them. Van had her bag stolen several times. When I think about that happening I get terribly worried."

Tuong found his own heart was pounding with anxiety. The words he used to console Hoa were also directed to himself: "Maybe Uncle Chinh takes her to and from school."

He stood up and put the newly painted sign on the wardrobe to dry. Hoa stood as well.

"Tuong, yesterday, Mr. Luan, the director of the municipal export company called and informed me he's coming to Cat Bac today. He wants to study the production potential of each district so he can make a report at the upcoming Municipal Party Congress. He and his staff may go out to the forestry station this afternoon. Get ready so you can go out with me to meet them and attest to the extent of our business operations."

Luan and his entourage arrived around ten in the morning. A blue Toyota sped up the road leading to the company offices, and the driver made a screeching circle in front of the building and then parked, almost defiantly, directly in front of the office door, as if vicariously enjoying his boss's power. Luan himself, a well-dressed man in his forties, stepped importantly out of the car. He shook hands with Hoa without warmth, but seriously and sternly, as if to establish his higher stature. Tuong was standing beside Hoa. When he saw Luan's eyes turn towards him, he stepped forward and extended his hand as well. But Luan deliberately turned away, putting one hand on Hoa's shoulder, and the two men walked into the office.

A young man, as well-dressed as Luan, scampered behind, carrying Luan's briefcase. When he caught up, Hoa glanced at him quickly. He felt a wave of surprise and nodded at the man.

"Quy. I'm sorry I didn't recognize you."

The two shook hands warmly.

"You two know each other?" Luan asked. He sat down and shook out a More cigarette from the pack on the table, then lit it. Exhaling with satisfaction, he gestured at the other man. "This is Quy. He got into some trouble when he was working as the economic engineer at the frozen seafood factory, so now he's asked to be my assistant. Be patient," he said, turning to Quy. "If the company expands and prospers, I'll make your family wealthy, right?"

Quy sat beside Hoa, glancing over at his boss.

"Yesterday, when my boss mentioned a man named Hoa," he whispered, "I knew immediately it was you. I would have said something to you before, but this new boss hates any interruptions while he's working."

"I thought you'd made your way back to Hanoi a long time ago. What happened to your uncle, the one who used to work for the General Staff?"

"God, talking about my uncle makes me sad," Quy said, shaking his head in exasperation. "When I was assigned to this place eight years ago, my uncle was on his tour abroad. When he came back, he asked me to be patient and work here for a few years, and then he would ask that I be reassigned to Hanoi. But he passed away a year later. So now I'm stuck here . . ."

Quy didn't need to remind Hoa about his situation with his uncle. When he was Hoa's classmate at college, Quy never cared much for studying. On his entrance exam, he had missed the cutoff grade by one point, but his uncle had pulled the appropriate strings so Quy could attend. For someone like him to get a choice post in Hanoi was not difficult at all. Since college, Hoa had tried to avoid him. He didn't like parasites who hid themselves in the shadows others cast. His principle was to live on his own abilities: only that way would he have the right to be proud of himself.

Later, when it was learned that Quy had been assigned to a remote area, everyone was shocked. Was it possible that his big-shot uncle had finally recognized his errors and had gotten serious about Quy? But no one had enough time or energy or interest to search out the truth. Hoa and Quy hadn't seen each other since then, eight years ago. Now Hoa knew what had happened.

He spoke politely with Quy. He still felt no sympathy for the man. But as he watched Quy trot after Luan, nodding and speaking obsequiously, he sensed a sadness in his old classmate—the sadness of someone who never developed into his own person, who had come to realize he had no one, not even himself, to rely on. Hoa felt sorry for him.

"I want to speak to you about increasing pork production for the municipal export company," Luan said, smashing the rest of his cigarette into the ashtray. "Until now, the quantity of pork from your company occupied a percentage of . . . what was the percentage, Quy?"

"Just a minute. Here you are," Quy said, startled, nervously opening a notebook. "The quantity of pork for export from the Cat Bac Export Company occupied 16 percent of the total amount from the whole city."

He said this rather pompously, as if to demonstrate the importance of his position to Hoa. But Hoa felt this only made him humiliate himself more. He began to feel more embarrassment than pity for the man.

The talk went on until lunch time. Tuong and the other staff of the company went to another room. Hoa, Luan, and two cadres from the district People's Committee remained in the front office. Quy hesitated, not knowing whether to stay or go, until Luan waved his hand at him. "Go have lunch with the drivers and other staff."

Quy paled. Seeing his humiliation, Hoa took his hand. "Please stay with me. We haven't seen each other in such a long time."

He made his tone very intimate, as if he were talking to a close friend—though all he really wanted to do was get Quy out of an embarrassing situation. Like a drowning person being rescued, Quy scampered over to Hoa and sat down beside him.

Hoa knew too well the way Quy thought. At the beginning of the meeting, he had felt a bit smug, pleased with himself. But then the dark cloud of a memory shadowed his thoughts. Quy's attitude depressed him. He remembered when he had first been transferred from the Agro-Forestry Department to take over the directorship of this company. He'd been shocked to discover that the storage area was just a cluster of low, thatched-roof huts situated on a muddy patch of land that was often flooded during the rainy season. The huts were narrow and dark and leaked everywhere. They looked as if they would collapse at the slightest touch. It was only the following year that the company had obtained the right to do self-accounting and active trading and so started to make a profit. At that point, he encouraged his staff to start building new offices and storage facilities. A few years later the company was making 150 percent of its projected profit, and the staff had built the blocks of collective flats. His workers were happy and satisfied; they worked enthusiastically, and everything improved greatly. It all hadn't happened by chance, and Hoa didn't think his pride in his accomplishments was unreasonable. But it made him sad to think about Quy, who felt the only way to succeed was by clinging to someone else's prestige and power. There were still too many people like him, with no desire to affirm their own abilities.

That afternoon, on their way to the state forestry enterprise, Hoa asked the driver to stop at Bua Gorge so he could show Luan the Tung Cau Cave. The group stood in front of the entrance, looking into the dark, deep interior. Luan glanced down at the slippery rocks, then said nonchalantly: "Pretty dark, isn't it? Quy, why don't you go down there and check it out for us before we go inside."

"Yes, yes, right away," Quy said, hurriedly tucking his bag under his arm and getting ready to descend.

But before he could move, a worker made a torch and walked in front to lead the way. Quy followed him down the wet, rocky slope, his steps jerky and hesitant. From above, Hoa could only see his miserable, bent back.

FIVE

News of Luyen's pregnancy quickly reached the headquarters of the state forestry enterprise.

The deputy director, Mr. Quan, found himself without the support of the director, who chose to avoid dealing with the issue and promptly passed responsibility for the matter on to his subordinate. Quan, full of resolve, arranged a meeting with the head of the Women's Union and the secretary of the Youth Union. The secretary was a man in his early twenties who blushed whenever anything dealing with women's problems were raised, a habit which kept him blushing constantly through staff meetings, since most of the staff were female. When the secretary saw an extremely angry Quan barreling towards his office, he immediately cajoled his deputy to go out to meet him, then escaped out of the back door. Miss Hao, the deputy secretary, was glad to run interference. She'd been waiting for an opportunity to demonstrate she was more capable and positive than her misogynistic boss, and happily agreed to Quan's suggestion that a meeting be held to discuss Luyen's condition.

At the meeting, Quan did not conceal his fury in front of Hao and Mrs. Diep, the head of the Women's Union.

"I'm 99 percent certain it was Mr. Vien who got Miss Luyen pregnant. I know him too well—he's a womanizer, and living among a group of young women, how could he be expected not to scratch his itch for sex?" Quan paused for a moment, realizing that perhaps he had said too much. "Well, who else could it be?" he asked. "To the west is the sea, and surrounding the camp is the forbidden jungle. Do you suppose some daring pilot parachuted in and screwed her for one night, then took off again? There's no question—I'd bet my mother's soul it was Vien."

"But . . ." Hao said hesitatingly, ". . . what if Miss Luyen . . . has . . . with Mr. Cuong?"

Quan's rejection of this idea was vehement. "Cuong is married to Mrs. Tham, a healthy, attractive woman. Don't you think she's enough for him? Anyway, how much damage do you really think that dwarf could do—he barely comes up to Luyen's ear. No, we must chastise Miss Luyen in a public meeting, so Vien's part in this can come out."

The more Quan said, the more he was coming to realize there was no way to speak of this matter in delicate terms. Miss Hao, who was a bit scandalized by the conversation at first, braced herself with the thought that challenging issues like the one at hand required strength and toughness of character, and she would do what she had to do to fulfill her duty.

Their determination to discover the truth of the matter now inflamed the three cadres with a fiery resolve. They marched vigorously through the jungle to Viet Hoa, determined to hover over Brigade Five like hawks until they detected the truth.

The public criticism of Luyen was held in the makeshift house belonging to the production brigade. The meeting opened with Luyen reading a self-criticism (required by her superiors) in which she detailed all her mistakes, took full responsibility for the matter, and declared her willingness to take any punishment given. She had no sooner folded the report and sat down when Quan leaned across the table and shouted:

"Who encouraged you to write that garbage? You go on at length about your errors, but you fail to mention the key issue. All we want to know is this—who got you pregnant? It's very simple."

Quan's question seemed appropriate enough under the circumstances, but what he secretly desired out of this affair was a way to attack his rival, Mr. Vien. Vien was secretary of the Brigade Five Party Cell and Quan was still furious with him for questioning Quan's "shoddy recruiting practices" during a meeting of the Party Committee last year. He knew Vien's intention had been to push him, Quan, out of his present position as deputy director by insinuating he was guilty of nepotism and taking bribes. Now Quan thought smugly of the common platitude: If you take off his shirt, everyone has a scar on his back—everyone has mistakes in his past. He'd taken this case precisely so he could reveal Vien's sinful back. Look at the man now, sitting there pretending to be calm, his face unnaturally placid. Unbearable!

"It doesn't matter who got me pregnant!" Luyen stood up suddenly, avoiding the stares of her colleagues. Her voice trembled and she seemed on the verge of tears. "Why do you want to know? Isn't it enough for you to humiliate me?"

Her last sentence caught the attention of Mrs. Diep, the head of the Women's Union, who told herself it was time to do her duty.

"Do you have any problems here? If there's anything wrong, please tell us and we'll try to find a way to help you."

The women of Brigade Five burst into bitter laughter.

"Can you help us get married or have children?" one asked loudly.

Her bluntness put the leaders in a difficult position. It was a delicate matter to criticize one's subordinates. Quan, disturbed by the impudence of the question, tapped the end of his pen against the table.

"We acknowledge your wish, comrades. But that isn't an issue to be discussed at this meeting. I'd like to reiterate that the aim of this gathering is to criticize the immoral, unethical and destructive behavior displayed by Luyen. Now—tell us, clearly and truthfully—who is the father of your child?"

Quan glanced covertly at Vien, victory in his heart. Sooner or later, he'd get the man.

"It's just like an opera, isn't it?" another girl asked loudly. "The village elder punishing the pregnant, unmarried girl."*

Quan beat his palm furiously against the side of the table, then whirled around and glared at the woman who had just dared to make that comparison.

*Refers to a popular Vietnamese opera in which such a girl is punished by village leaders who are blind, deaf, and dumb.

"Miss Bao, it has come to my attention that you are running off at the mouth. Who do you think we are—a group of blind, deaf, and dumb village mandarins? What a rude girl you are. Better watch your mouth."

Bao stood up and began shouting fiercely. "Why should I watch what I say? I'm pregnant too—how do you like that? Do you want to cross-examine me too?" Her anger dissipated as she looked around at her laughing colleagues. After a minute she continued, more calmly now, but still loudly and with passion. "I think this meeting is ridiculous. Humiliating this poor girl, interrogating her about who the 'culprit' is. If you comrades want the truth, why didn't you ask Luyen in private? All of us have known about her pregnancy for some time, but we've never questioned her."

Often, sincere words from a normally flippant, loud-mouthed person can be more persuasive than words spoken by another. But even these words from Bao didn't convince Quan to relent. He still felt Vien's shadow over him, and Bao's words only infuriated him more.

"The reason you've hidden her guilt and protected her is you'd all do the same as her if you had the chance. My God, everything has gone to hell here!"

A young woman with a sorrowful face and a fresh, maidenly appearance stood up. "I demand that comrade Quan keep a decent tongue in his head. Comrade, you scream, you scold, you criticize, you interrogate . . . but you don't take any time to find out the reality of the situation. We don't protect or even tolerate people who go overboard in their behavior. But at the same time we are not as heartless and unforgiving as you are towards someone who has made mistakes. Comrade, you should calm yourself, go sit by yourself for a moment, and close your eyes. Imagine if Brigade Five were made up entirely of single men rather than single women. And try to imagine you are one of those single men. Maybe you would clench your teeth and suffer and overcome your natural desires and the need for love—as I have. But many others can't do that. And if a person does, what does she have left as her reward? No family, and not even a child to console her."

The last word seemed like the final stone holding out in a dam about to burst. The young woman intended to continue, but her voice failed her and she sat down.

Even Quan was moved by her words. But he refused to forget his original goal. When he spoke, he mumbled, almost to himself: "So you're saying if we want to show our compassion for you, we must bring in a group of men to inseminate you? Ladies, in a herd of goats, only one male is necessary!"

Mien had not intended to speak, but Quan's vulgar words brought her to her feet, shouting: "Comrade Deputy Director. Please don't abuse us like that!" She stressed the word "us" with a heavy, trembling tone, as if her voice were weighed down by a huge rock. "I want to tell you about myself, so that perhaps you can understand us better. I was born in the Year of the Goat, 1943, so I am now forty-two. During the American War, I was the commander of a Volunteer Youth platoon which was based in Tung Cau Cave, at the top of Bua Gorge. It is named that because the summit is very high, and as you reach it, along the curving road, you feel haunted, as if you were truly under the spell of some witchcraft.* Back then, it was just a dirt trail, not paved as it is now. On one side is the slope of the mountain, and on the other, as you know, is a deep ravine. We split that mountain, blew up the rocks, and built a network of roads that extended all over this island. We were all young girls, but we were virtually without individual desires. At that time, we were absolutely dedicated to only one goal—defeating the enemy and obtaining peace. Once we had peace, we thought, then we'd have everything else . . . a husband, children . . ."

Mien was silent for a long time. Behind the house, a hen cackled as she laid an egg. Mien looked at Quan. He seemed to be listening nervously, but his face was still stubborn and impassive.

"After 1973, our regiment was moved here to build the state forestry enterprise. Many of us in Brigade Five now were part of my wartime platoon. We have peace now, but the men we were waiting for never returned. During the American War, we lived at the edge of death, and we were able to control our instinctual desires. But now such control is impossible. I know I lost my opportunity to get married. But if at least I had a child, I would be consoled in many ways. If I hadn't been so concerned with 'preserving' myself all those years ago, at least I could have had a child with my beloved. And at least I wouldn't have to suffer like I do now. But he's dead, with all the rest, and who did I keep myself for? What do I need with my virginity, when all it does is bring me loneliness? The col-

**Bua* means witchcraft.

lective can help me strengthen my willpower, it can console me a bit. But the collective can't bring me private happiness."

At this point, everyone expected Mien to conclude with something like, "that's why I think . . ." and return to the problem of Luyen. But Mien sat down silently. She refused to cry, but her face was suffused with sadness. She didn't dare speak for Luyen's feelings. No, she was speaking for herself. One day a public criticism like this could be directed at her. Her co-workers in the production brigade weren't aware, but lately she had begun experiencing emotions and desires she had never felt before. Maybe Luyen had felt the same way, or sensed it in her, because she'd asked Mien to go with her to the western slope of the mountain, and there admitted all the facts about her pregnancy. Mien's bed was next to hers. Before she'd revealed the truth, Luyen had begun complaining that she felt uneasy and a little nauseous. Then one day Mien had seen her hiding some wild tamarind fruits, round and green as marble, under her pillow.* At times also Luyen would vomit, though she tried not to let anyone see. Mien herself didn't know anything about the symptoms of pregnancy, but she had had some limited experience taking care of her sister years before, and grew suspicious as she looked at Luyen's straight, stiff back and heavy walk. One day, when there was no one else in the barracks, Luyen had hugged Mien tightly and burst into tears. Mien unbuttoned Luyen's baggy blouse and looked at her swollen breasts and her dark nipples. That was all the proof she'd needed.

*When a woman desires sour-tasting foods like tamarind fruits, it is taken as a sign that she is pregnant.

Once she knew the truth, she was both jealous and worried for Luyen. And for herself too. Perhaps what she knew now would draw her to the beach as well, to wait for that young man, to repeat Luyen's fate. She had wanted for too long to have a child of her own.

What she didn't anticipate was the effect her words would have on her colleagues assembled in the large, makeshift house. Quan's face had grown redder as she spoke, and he was more agitated than ever. He punched the table and screamed as if he had lost his senses completely. The women grew frightened at his fury, but they remained quiet and waited for him to cool down, so they could resume their discussion, make him understand them.

"Luyen, I will ask you one more time!" Quan roared. "WHO GOT YOU PREGNANT?"

Luyen felt intimidated by Quan's unexpected fury. She looked beseechingly to Mien for help. But despite being head of the production brigade, Mien felt she still didn't have enough power to protect Luyen as well as herself. She remained silent.

"Fine, be stubborn, Miss Luyen. But your will can never compete with mine. Cuong, where the hell are you?" Quan whirled around, piercing Cuong with a stare that went through him like a bullet. Oh God, he thought. Is he going to blame me for her pregnancy? His little legs twitched nervously. "Cuong, what the hell are you doing?" Quan yelled again. "Take Miss Luyen into the storage shed and keep her there until she decides to confess who the father of her child is. She will be released only on my orders, do you understand? And if you don't watch her well, you'll have me to deal with—is that clear?"

All the women leapt to their feet, shocked. In less than an hour Quan had become a brutal dictator. A pale Mrs. Diep tugged hesitatingly at his sleeve.

"Sir, I really don't think we should do this."

Quan whipped his arm away and glared at her as if he were ready to eat her alive. "Don't you tell me what to do, Mrs. Diep! Who do you think is in charge here? By noon, she'll be so hungry she'll be ready to point the finger at Vien, and I'll release her as soon as she confesses." He spun again. "Cuong, what the hell are you doing? You're slow as a dying rooster."

Cuong, white-faced, scurried over to Quan. He took Luyen's arm gently, silently begging her to go without making a fuss. They walked together to the storage shed, the small man next to the tall woman. Both were trembling. Cuong could barely control his fear. What if he were fingered as the father of Luyen's child? He and Vien were the only men in Brigade Five. Who else could it be? Quan stomped after the two of them, holding his hands behind him, alternately clasping them and kneading his buttocks.

❧

At noon, just as Quan was about to take a nap, a timid Cuong approached his bed.

"Dear sir, the women wish to bring lunch to Luyen."

Quan shot up. "You will not permit them to go to her. No

one is allowed to bring her food. She'll have to go hungry until two this afternoon, and then she'll be forced to make her statement."

He glanced at his watch, grunted a few times in satisfaction, then lay down again. He fantasized about the moment he would have Vien's fate in his hands. This time the one who liked to criticize and accuse would be the one who was smashed! This time Vien would be the one punished, would surely lose his position as Party Cell secretary of Brigade Five. After all, Luyen was only a woman. She'd been very tough at the beginning, but by the end of the meeting she'd collapsed like the fur on a soaked cat. By two, she'd surely confess. Years ago, when he'd commanded an engineering battalion, there'd been a soldier who was suspected of stealing a watch from one of his comrades. He'd ordered his men to tie up the man and put him in a storage shed overnight. By the next morning, the thief had confessed to everything. Luyen was only a woman—it surely wouldn't take as long to break her down.

But by six in the evening Luyen still hadn't broken her silence. Quan was furious, but his determination remained strong. "No problem," he said to Mrs. Diep and Miss Hao. "Let her stay there overnight. My former soldiers were more stubborn than her, but I managed to reeducate them. By six tomorrow morning, once she confesses and the whole matter is resolved, we'll go back to headquarters."

He tapped the face of his watch confidently and returned to his room.

Cuong spent the night in the room next to the storage shed. He usually took his responsibilities to heart out of fear of punishment; he was a weak man, both physically and spiritually. Just listening to harsh words and loud voices made him feel dizzy. Earlier that day, he'd vowed to himself to stay up all night in order to fulfill his duties as guard. But Miss Bao, unimpressed, brought Luyen her dinner. "Just be careful," she told him. "If you dare report this to Mr. Quan, just remember that he's only going to be here a few days, and then he'll go back to headquarters. But you're here every day, all day. We can destroy your whole rotten lineage, from the roots to the top."

There was no doubt that she was the fiercest woman in Brigade Five. He had tried to prevent her from bringing food to Luyen, but Bao's yells had hit him in the face like a blow and he found himself meekly opening the door for her. Loudmouthed people always intimidated him. After that incident, he told himself there was no use in his staying up all night. Despite his being there, Luyen's friends brought her a mosquito net and a mat. There she was, imprisoned, but sleeping on a proper mat with mosquito netting around it, just as if she were on holiday in a guest house.

And so Quan's plan to return to the state forestry enterprise's headquarters with a signed confession from Luyen and Mr. Vien was not realized. The next morning, when he walked over to the storage shed and peered through the window at Luyen, he was infuriated to see her rolling up her mat and folding her mosquito net. He whirled around to face Cuong, then heard Luyen call to Cuong, asking him to let her out so she could go to the toilet. Cuong, terrified, didn't answer, but looked at Quan.

"You're not leaving this room until you confess!" Quan

shouted. More delay was unbearable . . . but what could he do? Despite his bravado, he knew deep inside that he lacked true strength and resolve. Until now he hadn't doubted that Luyen and Mr. Vien would have to submit to him. Luyen had been starved and imprisoned for almost a full day; surely she'd confess by noon.

But the members of Brigade Five had decided that their suffering and humiliation at the hands of comrade Quan were at an end. Quan may have been in the military, but the majority of the women had been in the Volunteer Youth brigades themselves. They'd survived bombs and bullets, jungle rains and rugged mountains, and they'd risked their lives to do whatever had been asked of them, from building roads to shooting down American aircraft. Their experiences had taught them to obey orders, but their experiences also taught them not to follow the wrong-headed caprices of a dictatorial, hateful bully. When Quan had ordered Luyen confined to the storage shed, the women had hesitated to protest, since he was their leader and they all had remnants of respect for his position. But now the situation had gotten ridiculous. Quan's senseless cruelty forfeited any right he may have had to be respected.

At noon, as Cuong sat half-dozing in front of the shed, he was startled to see a mob of women marching towards him. He leapt to his feet, then leaned against the door of the shed, his right hand buried deep in his trouser pocket, clutching his keys.

"Cuong, open that door and let Luyen out," Bao said, not bothering with formalities. "One day of humiliation is enough."

Cuong glanced once at Bao's tough face and fought down

his panic. He felt dizzy; all he wanted to do was run away. But then he thought of Quan's angry red face and couldn't move.

"Impossible," he whispered nervously.

The semicircle of women tightened closer around him. Bao thrust her finger at his belly like a dagger. "If you're afraid to open it, then give me your keys."

His keys? As storage keeper, his only power lay in those keys. At home, his mother browbeat him and he felt powerless around his wife. His only strength lay in his control of the production team's storage rooms. He fretted and worried endlessly about his duties, and guarded his keys with his life. No one had ever dared to touch them before. Now Bao demanded that they be turned over to her! What could he do? If he refused to give them to her, these women would tear him to pieces. Who would protect him from them?

"Impossible," he moaned, almost begging. He glanced over his shoulder, looking for any kind of help.

"Do I have to take them by force?" Bao yelled, leaping forward as if she meant to plough into him head on.

Terrified, Cuong slipped away from the door and started to run. But he was too slow. After he'd taken a few steps, he felt a pair of determined arms grasp him around the waist. The women swarmed in, surrounding him, pulling him to and fro, pecking at him like chickens fighting over a grain of rice. Miss Bao seized his hand and swung him around in a circle. Dizzy, he tripped over his own feet and fell. Bao yanked his hand out of his pocket, pried open his fingers and snatched the ring of keys. The exultant women towered over his curled body on the ground.

"Will you run away now and report this to your dear Mr. Quan?" one yelled.

"Throw him in the shed!" said another. "How many times did you run and tattle to dear Mr. Quan yesterday, Cuong?"

Cuong rose unsteadily to his feet. In his fear and confusion, he was only aware of a jumble of colors and a babble of voices around him. Then, quite clearly, he saw Luyen walk triumphantly out of the storage shed. Before he could utter one cry of protest, Bao pushed him inside and slammed the door behind him.

The women took Luyen by her arms and pulled her along as they ran across the large yard. A flock of pecking chickens squawked and flapped in terror as they rushed by. They didn't stop until they were at Quan's door.

"Mr. Quan, you've had your fun, but now it's all over!" Bao shouted angrily. "We aren't sheep for you to pen up and punish according to your mood. We've had enough! No one in Brigade Five will tell you a damn thing!"

"What we will do," another woman cried out, "is report your abusive behavior to the district level and make sure you're punished."

"Now get the hell out of here!" yelled Bao. Within seconds the entire group had dispersed, leaving Quan standing alone in the doorway of his room.

SIX

Tuong waded into the tank. The turtles hovered around his feet. He gently picked one up and laid it upside down, on its shell, in a bamboo basket. Then he stretched his arms over the rim of the tank and grabbed the scale. He hooked the basket onto it. The turtle weighed nearly one and a half kilos, almost one hundred grams heavier than it had been last month. Not bad for a year-old turtle in the cold season. Quite good in fact. He wiped his hands and noted the turtle's weight in the book he'd placed next to the tank. Methodically, he measured the length of the shell and the width of the neck opening, before placing the turtle back among its brothers and sisters.

As he climbed out of the tank, he spotted a small boat approaching the beach. When it was closer, he was surprised to see Hoa and Phuc. What would make Hoa come here, unexpected and unannounced?

"Good morning," he yelled, as he ran towards his friend, smiling to hide his uneasiness. "What brings you?"

"You're looking at the new head turtle breeder." Hoa laughed sardonically as he jumped onto the beach. He was carrying two overnight bags.

Tuong looked quizzically at Phuc. The man's lips were clamped tightly together, his face tense, as if he were trying to control a verbal or physical outburst. Deciding to hold his questions for the moment, Tuong bent down and grabbed one corner of the huge bag of rice Phuc was struggling out of the boat. He and Phuc carried the bag between them as the three men walked up the beach to the house.

When they arrived at the house, Phuc threw the bag of rice to the floor and shook his fist.

"You're too damn soft," he said. "Really, Hoa, tell me who did this to you and let me deal with him. I'll take full responsibility for it."

Hoa put his bags down on the bamboo bed, walked over to the tea table and poured a cup for Phuc. "Have some tea and forget about this revenge business. Do you remember when I first interviewed you for the company, and you told me how hot-tempered you were? Remember what you promised me?"

"How can I forget?" Phuc sheepishly avoided Hoa's gaze. "But this is unbearable!"

"Don't you think I feel anger too? Don't you think I'm suffering? But I refuse to retaliate to their injustice with violence. We're right and we'll be proven right. We just have to be patient and keep calm . . ."

Tuong slowly learned what had happened. Shortly before, there had been an internal upheaval in the local People's Committee. The old leadership was ousted, and the new leadership decided that restructuring was needed in certain departments. Hoa's export company had been the target of many accusations and allegations by a few committee members, and also by some people from other departments who were suspicious or jealous of the company's success. The new leadership decided to remove Hoa as director while the investigations were underway. Mr. Dan had been assigned as acting director, and Hoa was sent to the turtle breeding camp.

Of course everyone understood that the changes were based on personal vendettas rather than logic or sound business practices. Hoa knew he could protest both the investigation and his reassignment by the People's Committee and demand to be returned to his position. But he didn't. Instead, he quietly transferred his duties to Dan and ignored the staff's agitation and anger. For days, all they did was whisper to each other in corners of the office, hardly bothering with their work. All of them liked Hoa, and most felt grateful and indebted to him for giving them second chances. How could they not protest his banishment in some way? The night before he was going to demand to be told the real reason for his sacking, a group of the more hot-tempered employees came to his room. "Tell me who's responsible for this ridiculous decision and I'll take care of him myself," Phuc told him.

Hoa had been touched by their loyalty, but he just shook his head slowly. "If I'm innocent, the facts will prove it," he said firmly. "I hope you'll all continue to do good work here and not try to sabotage either your job or the welfare of the company because you feel I've been wronged. Keep working hard and keep being honest—that's the best way to support me. We all have to control our anger and be as patient as we can."

He had looked straight into Dai's eyes, and Nu's, and Phuc's, and the rest of the worried eyes in that room. As he'd watched those eyes grow less anxious, Hoa had felt at peace with himself.

Phuc listened to Hoa now, his face clouded.

Hoa looked around the room, searching for a way to change the subject. He was startled to see several paintings of nude women propped in the corner near Tuong's bed. He walked over to inspect them. They were newly painted. In one, a naked woman was reclining against some pillows on Tuong's bamboo bed, her hand resting softly against her cheek. In another, the same girl, still naked, leaned against a rock on a deserted beach.

Hoa looked up to see Tuong standing beside him, blushing, clearly anticipating Hoa's reaction. Hoa straightened and smiled, but his expression was severe.

"It's not an easy thing, painting a nude," he said. "It's hard to know how to make it a tribute to the natural and sacred beauty of human beings, and not just arouse carnal lust." He looked at the two paintings again. "I'm afraid you've done something a true artist should avoid, Tuong."

His annoyance seemed not directed at Tuong's decadence or desires, but it was as if he felt Tuong was betraying his talent, as if it hurt him that someone whose work he admired and respected so much had painted something lewd and common.

He bent his head, as if he were the one humiliated. Tuong stood next to him, nervously rubbing his hands behind his back. He understood what Hoa meant, but didn't know how to reassure his friend. Finally, he bent down and turned the paintings to the wall. As he turned, he saw Hoa examining the calendar on Tuong's bed. The words "To give birth to a son or daughter as one wishes" were written across the boxes for the 16th, 17th, and 18th of December.* Tuong snatched up the calendar and thrust it into his knapsack. But Hoa was staring at him.

The atmosphere was strained for the rest of the day. No one spoke, not even Phuc. It was unusually windy outside, and the bamboo walls and thatched roof of the simple house shook incessantly. Tuong desperately wanted to pry Hoa out of his silence, to chat about nothing or anything to lessen the tension. But Hoa remained silent. In just a short period of time, he had been forced out of his job and torn away from the people and the place he had grown to love. Now he'd realized that someone he liked and admired, someone he had put so much hope and trust into, had done something which was, to his mind and heart, completely unacceptable.

Phuc left that night. When he was gone, Tuong sat in a corner near a kerosene lamp, pretending to read a book. Hoa walked over to him, took his hand, and looked deep into his troubled eyes.

"You heard what I said to Phuc this morning, Tuong. If we want to prove who we are and what we believe in this life, we have to try hard, be patient, and not give in to instincts or desires that will only set us back."

Tuong sat motionless for a moment, then grasped his friend's

*Vietnamese newspapers sometimes publish auspicious days to conceive a male or female child.

hands fervently. He felt their intimacy and mutual respect had returned.

"Brother Hoa . . ." He wanted to say more. But he knew Hoa had heard all he needed to hear—Tuong's love, his gratitude, and his apology—in those two words.

He felt ashamed as he thought of all he had done in the last few months. His sexual desire had intensified to the point where he felt trapped in a crazy, churning circle. He had no time to think, to consider what he was doing or where he was going. Every once in a while he had thought of Van, imagining her steady gaze and honest eyes fixing him, demanding an explanation for his behavior. Now he saw Hoa's accusatory eyes as well, his gentle yet serious reprimand. He cursed himself and swore he would never return to that beach.

He had gone back many times, after his first encounter with Luyen in front of the cave. At first, he had been surprised to see that a zigzag path had been cut down the face of the formerly impassable mountain. He brought his paints and easel with him some time later, and was startled, though not surprised, to see a strange young woman sitting there. It didn't take much effort to persuade her to pose naked for him. This pattern continued over the next weeks, each time with a different woman, until finally he realized the place was no longer isolated or remote. He sensed, though he could not see, pair after pair of eyes, hidden behind the trees or among the flowers on the slope of the mountain, always staring with intense and unabashed yearning. After a time, he no longer only painted pictures of the women he met on the beach—he usually managed to persuade them to come back to the turtle breeding camp with him. He repeated this pattern with several different women. Many nights, after he had brought a woman back to the beach, he swore to himself that this would be the last time. But he'd only manage to keep his promise for a few days. Then the lust would rise again, and he'd let himself be carried on its wave.

By the time Hoa had been at the camp for a month, Tuong was as tense with desire as a kite string. As for Hoa, many nights he woke to the sound of Tuong tossing and turning on his bamboo bed, pulling on the jute mat, sometimes even biting his pillow.

He wasn't immune to Tuong's sufferings. At night, sometimes, he saw vague images before him: the brazenly naked bodies in Tuong's paintings. He'd seen many paintings of nudes before. Mostly they were Renaissance works: he loved the primal beauty they exuded, their sensual depictions of the fine muscle lines of the human body. But surely Tuong's paintings aroused an unnatural carnality. He shouldn't, couldn't, accept that purpose in art. But he was feverish, haunted by the paintings, as if they were ghosts or devils. Feelings he had thought he'd stifled were stirring in a dark, hidden corner of himself.

One night he dreamt a head was resting on his chest. At first it rested lightly, like a book. But then the pressure increased and the head became heavier, until it was hard for him to breath. It started thrashing back and forth wildly, pressing even more strongly into his chest, as if it were struggling to break free and liberate itself from whatever was holding it down.

The next morning, thinking of the dream, Hoa decided it

was caused by his obsession with the paintings and with Tuong's obvious suffering. He was a healthy, thirty-year-old bachelor; certainly such a dream was not out of the ordinary. But he couldn't deny to himself either that his desires had been stirred and agitated in a remarkably intense way since he'd moved to Yellow Cow Island.

❧

When Hoa was thirteen, his aunt gave birth to his cousin Van. His family was in difficult economic straits at the time, so at the start of the summer holidays, Hoa asked Uncle Chinh for help in finding a job. His uncle sent him to an acquaintance, a building contractor who accepted Hoa as his apprentice. At first Hoa followed his orders faithfully and worked hard. But the contractor was rude and harsh and their relationship grew tense.

One morning they went to repair a leaking tile roof. The contractor sat down and made himself comfortable at a tea table inside, lighting up a cigarette and relaxing. "Go up on the roof," he told Hoa, "and start breaking up the tiles."

His intention was to have Hoa locate the leak, smash the tiles around it, and rebuild the area to seal the leak. An hour later, when he climbed up to check Hoa's progress, he was shocked to see that Hoa had broken up most of the roof. He rushed over to his apprentice, grabbed his ear and twisted it, then screamed, "You idiot! What the hell are you doing—digging your father's grave?"

Hoa, furious, batted his boss's arm away and yelled, "Don't you dare mention my father! You told me to break up the tiles and I did! What else do you want?"

"You have the nerve to argue with me?" The contractor stared at Hoa. "Get the hell out of here! If I see you anywhere near me I'll beat the shit out of you."

The man was known to have a fierce temper, and the people who worked for him for a while usually got used to his screaming and threats. They knew eventually he'd calm down. Hoa knew it also. He understood that in a few hours his boss would call him and tell him to come back to work. But he'd had enough. He couldn't work with this man any more. He climbed down from the roof, grabbed the ladder and ran with it. Some distance away, he propped the ladder against a sapindus tree, waved at the contractor, and walked home, the echoes of the man's crazy shouts reverberating in his ears.

It was several more hours before the owner of the house returned and propped the ladder back against the roof so the red-faced contractor could finally descend. Raging, he rushed to Uncle Chinh's house and bellowed out the story. "I'm lucky that ignorant little bastard didn't throw me off the roof!" he shouted finally.

Uncle Chinh tried to calm him down, while simultaneously pushing him out of the house as quickly as he could. "Please go home, sir," he said. "And don't worry. I'll punish him."

After the contractor had departed, Uncle Chinh stood by the door, trembling with anger. He felt embarrassed and insulted. He had done his best to educate his nephew, yet Hoa had acted like an ignorant hooligan. When Hoa came out of his room, Uncle Chinh ordered him to stand facing the wall, then went outside and cut a section of bamboo.

"I'm going to make a whip," he declared angrily to Hoa, as he sat on a bench next to him.

Uncle Chinh had never raised a hand to Hoa; until now he'd never even needed to raise his voice in anger. Hoa risked a glance at him. His uncle had picked up a knife and appeared to be splitting the section of bamboo into a thin, painful strand. His face was hard and set, and the look in his eyes frightened Hoa. Yet he could see that behind Uncle Chinh's fierce appearance, he was straining mightily to control the anger that was coursing through him. He was making a whip to beat his nephew, yet with each stroke of the knife he seemed also to be pushing down a wild beast that threatened to spring out at any moment.

Why was he taking so long with the whip? Hoa grew more and more nervous and kept glancing at his uncle. The bamboo had been split to a very thin whip by now, one that would be extremely painful on his backside. His nerves were at the breaking point as he imagined the bamboo whistling through the air and landing on his defenseless buttocks. Why couldn't his uncle just get it over with? Bamboo shavings fell around his feet, some twisted into tiny springs, others shaped like little hooks. Minute after minute passed, until finally, desperately, Hoa turned to face his uncle.

The whip had been worried away until it was the size of a chopstick. Uncle Chinh broke what was left in two and stood up. His anger had faded. The many minutes he'd spent whittling the bamboo had given him the time he needed to control his anger. His nephew had made a mistake, but he knew also that the contractor had humiliated Hoa first and Hoa had merely reacted to protect his self-respect.

Through the years, Hoa had made more mistakes, and each time Uncle Chinh would sit down and begin making a bamboo whip, cutting and shaving in silence, until his anger was whittled away. He knew that beating Hoa was not the right solution. What was done was done. Better to wait for a more peaceful moment and then explain why what he'd done was wrong.

Now, nearly twenty years later, Hoa would still think of Uncle Chinh and his bamboo with a feeling of intense respect. He also had another memory that was particularly vivid for him. Once, at dinner, he had described how a classmate had a new motorbike and how he wished his family wasn't so poor, so they could buy one as well. Uncle Chinh listened and said nothing. But later that night, as the two men sat together drinking tea, he said: "People suffer because they desire what's not in their reach. You want a motorbike and you preoccupy yourself with finding a way to get one. Yet since you can't afford it, all you do is suffer and live in turmoil instead of peace. Just work hard and patiently and life will bring you no more or less than what you deserve."

Hoa had tried to live by his uncle's advice, and although it was difficult at times, over the years he had learned to develop an inner sense of peace and acceptance. He felt his life had been made easier as a result. He knew how to control the desire for material things, to be patient and work for what he wanted.

His uncle's insistence on developing Hoa's interest in cultural activities had also helped him. Uncle Chinh brought Hoa and Van with him to art exhibits, to films and the theater, and he often bought books for them. Later in his life, Hoa found that his greatest wish was the desire for a good book or a beautiful painting.

Uncle Chinh especially liked ancient Chinese poetry, which he would frequently recite to Hoa and Van, while explaining its sometimes complicated symbolism. Hoa and his cousin learned to appreciate and then to love the strange words Chinh would recite, finding in them a mysterious beauty. One particular poem that had become embedded in Hoa's memory went like this:

Quan tai Tuong giang dau
Thiep tai Tuong giang vi
Tuong co bat tuong kien
Dong am Tuong giang thuy.

You live upstream on the Tuong river,
Downstream on the Tuong river live I,
Each of us longs for, but cannot see the other
Though we drink the same Tuong river water.

Uncle Chinh explained: "The young man lived upstream on the Tuong, and his beloved was downstream from him.

Each longed for the other, and would think joyfully of the other, as they both drank from the same source. But they could never see each other. The poem expresses ambiguous and hopeless sorrow and nostalgia."

At the time, Hoa had been disappointed. "I don't get it. How does just drinking the same river water mean they love or miss each other that much?"

Uncle Chinh smiled slightly. "Read the poem again and think about it more carefully. It contains the ache of waiting. Drinking from the same source of water is both consolation and restriction, the boundary of an unrequited desire."

That emphasis on control and acceptance was why Uncle Chinh liked the poem. And although many years had passed, Hoa still knew it by heart. Whenever he thought of it, he imagined a river—no, an immense sea, separating the mainland from his island.

❧

Hoa explained to Tuong that he tended to separate women into two basic categories: mother-types and sister-types. Most younger women reminded him of his cousin Van and he tended to feel protective towards them. As for those women he encountered, mostly through his company, who had made some kind of "mistake" in their pasts—he felt empathy for them, but never disdain.

Once when he was a small boy, he'd awakened to hear his mother arguing in low tones with a strange woman. He couldn't hear the stranger's exact words, even though her voice was sharp and piercing as a needle. But he heard his mother's determined reply:

"Your proposal is impossible. Yes, if I take up your offer I can make good money. But I'll lose my children's respect. Yes, strangers wouldn't know who I am. But I won't shame myself in front of my children . . . I can't do what you're asking."

After the woman had gone, Hoa sprang up and hugged his mother. Why was she crying? Widowed at thirty-six, she refused to marry again, fearing her four children would suffer with a new father. He always remembered his mother's face that night, suffused with purity and wisdom.

Another corner of his heart was always reserved for little Van, a part of him that was fresh and pure and that helped him when his soul felt weighted with darkness. Two years before, when he'd gone back to Hanoi for his annual vacation, Van was just starting to grow into her nascent beauty—the proverbial bud just beginning to blossom. She was in the eighth grade at the time, and in the evening was taking extra classes to improve her skills. Hoa would wait at the front gate for her to return. But one evening she was late. Hoa stood, tapping his fingers nervously against the gate post. Suddenly Van tore around the corner, peddling her bicycle furiously, as if she were being chased. As soon as she reached the gate, she jumped off her bike and let it fall to the ground, then grabbed her cousin and burst into tears, her whole body trembling uncontrollably. Hoa finally managed to calm her down, and she told him what happened. When she had turned the corner onto the long street that led home, a gang of teenage boys had sprung out of the darkness and attacked her. They snatched her books, pulled her hair, and groped at her young body, laughing cruelly at her. Finally, she'd managed to get on her bicycle and get away, but they yelled to her that she had to come back to them the next night if she wanted her books back.

Hoa smoothed her hair and kneaded her shoulders. "Don't cry, cousin. You have to be tough. Look, starting tomorrow, I'll come to your school and ride back with you."

Suddenly, a burst of raucous laughter, followed by a blast of loud music came from the apartment above Van's. Van shuddered. "Boys like that are everywhere."

"I'll come pick you up," Hoa simply repeated.

The next evening, as promised, he did. As they turned the dark corner onto the street where Van had been attacked the night before, Hoa saw the gang waiting near some aged sapindus trees. Without any hesitation, he walked up to them, his face cold and expressionless. In a low, even voice, he told the boys to return Van's books. Hoa's demeanor and self-confidence chilled the teenagers. They grudgingly returned the books. Looking at them, Hoa found himself surprised at the brutality stamped on their faces. Who were these kids? Didn't they have mothers, or sisters like Van?

From that day, he took her to and from school, and arranged for Uncle Chinh to take over those duties when he had to return to Cat Bac Island. One evening, just before he went back, he walked as usual to the school to meet Van. She had mentioned that class might be let out early that night, and Hoa had told her to wait among the group of students who tended to gather after class. As he approached the dark corner where Van had been attacked, he heard a girl scream, then whimper pitifully. His heart leapt and he raced towards the voice. Why hadn't she waited for him in front of the school, as he'd told her? As he reached the corner, he realized that it wasn't Van. Another young woman was being held tightly by one boy as a second tried to pry her handbag from her fingers. Hoa rushed over, grabbed the nearest boy by the back of his shirt, swung him around and punched him in the face. He ducked quickly to avoid a roundhouse swing by another boy, then sprang back up and chopped him in the neck with the side of his hand. He had time to sweep out his leg and trip the first boy before a blow from behind rammed him into the gnarled trunk of one of the sapindus trees.

A whistle sounded, followed by the sound of running footsteps.

"Cops! Let's get the hell out of here!" one of the teenagers shouted. The gang scattered in various directions.

Hoa didn't particularly want to deal with the police either; he needed to find Van. He got quickly to his feet, looking around, noticing that the young woman must have escaped during the fight. He half-trotted down the dark street, searching the shadows for his cousin.

"Brother . . ." The whispered word made him jump. He turned and saw the woman he'd rescued peering over a low retaining wall.

"You should go home," he said gently, to her terrified face. "Next time, avoid this street. It's a dangerous place for a woman walking alone."

"How can I avoid it," the young woman asked bitterly. "I

work the afternoon shift and this is the time we finish. If I take Bach Mai Street, it'll add an extra two kilometers to my walk." She stared at Hoa and her bitterness turned to concern. "Brother, you're bleeding."

He hadn't noticed the cut before, but at her words he became aware of a warm, wet trail easing down his neck. He took his handkerchief from his pocket and dabbed at the wound. The woman pulled her bicycle out from behind the wall and walked along with him. They both lamented about the sorry state things had come to, that a young woman couldn't walk safely down the street.

"I should have become a teacher," she said. "I passed the entrance exam for teachers' college, but I didn't enjoy teaching and decided to be a worker instead. But maybe if there were one more teacher to show these kids a better way to act, we might have one less lost person."

This first encounter developed into a friendship between Hoa and the young woman, and when he returned to Cat Bac Island, she wrote to him often. But he was hesitant to get too deeply involved with her, as kind and intelligent as he found her to be. He understood that a romantic relationship couldn't survive the long distance, and he knew she'd never come to the island with him. Yet every time he thought of her, or of his cousin Van, walking down that long, empty, dark street, his heart would pound and a weight would settle on his chest. Things needed to change. Van and the young woman weren't the only ones who needed help, he said to Tuong. Society was failing those boys as well.

On the night Tuong heard these stories, all the memories of Van that he had tried to stifle were awakened in him. As he thought of her, he felt a sharp pang of guilt. Would she feel proud of what he'd been doing now?

"I don't understand the kind of man who treats women badly," Hoa said, still lost in his own memories. "I hate men who behave brutally, rudely to women. They're our mothers and sisters, not strangers. If they've made mistakes or been unlucky, they should be helped, not abused."

Was this a message directed at him? Previously Tuong would have agreed with Hoa, taken what he said at face value. But now, after several days of wrestling with his desires and his guilt, he looked at Hoa with suspicion. If Hoa felt all women were his mother or sister, did that mean he'd never touched a woman, let alone satisfied her, brought her to the throes of orgasm? As he looked into Hoa's clear eyes and sincere face, he thought he understood all. Fine. Let him be a saint. But did he have to impose his ideas of chastity on other people? Did he have to try to extinguish everyone else's sexual desires?

What he didn't know was that every third or fourth night, Hoa would again experience the same ghastly nightmare. The ghost would glide to his bed, kneel next to it, put its head on his chest. Soon the head would begin to moan and harangue him, demanding to be released so it could move around freely. Hoa would feel his whole body pressed back into the bed, heavy and paralyzed with terror.

One morning, after the nightmare, Hoa remembered with a sense of sick horror how he could feel a small, tumor-like object, the size of a tiny green pea, when the head pressed itself against his naked chest. Looking across to the other bed, he noticed that on Tuong's cheek was a small, raised mole with a short hair growing out of it. He shook his head and tried to clear his mind. These nightmares were driving him crazy.

SEVEN

The French invaders had besieged the cave for weeks, until they were certain all of Tan Dac's guerillas hiding inside were dead. During those days of siege, the wife of the unlucky old man who'd been beheaded had a recurring dream in which she saw a cave filled with the spirits of the dead, saw them seeping out through cracks in the rocks and gathering in a white mist in a dark corner of the forest. Afterwards, night after night, her brave, beheaded grandson appeared in her dreams as well, sobbing bitterly and screaming: "Tell me, grandma, can a head be reattached to a body? Can it? Can it? Can it?"

At her tea stall, the old woman began to ask the customers that same question: "Can a head be reattached to a body?"

Their response was invariably the same. "Of course not."

One night, her grandson appeared again in her dream. But instead of screaming about his detached head, he said calmly: "Grandma, I'm coming to see you tomorrow."

By morning, the old woman forgot the dream. She woke and began to prepare a pot of sticky rice to sell for the morning meal. But no matter how much wood she placed on the fire, no matter how long she kept the pot on the flames, the rice simply would not cook. Suddenly, she remembered her grandson's words in her dream. Leaving the rice, she ran wildly out of her tiny house and into the main road. A whirlwind howled above her head. Looking up into it, she saw a head swirling around inside the cone of wind. A tree branch, torn off by the force of the whirlwind, circled madly around the head like a single spoke. At once, the wind died and the head and the branch fell to the ground near her feet, with a sickening thud.

Years later, her second grandson—the one who had survived Tan Dac's massacre of his loved ones and then, to avenge their deaths, had gone to work as a scout for the French—came home. It wasn't long afterwards that he came down with an unknown disease that slowly, inexorably, drove him mad. One day, he went to visit the grave where his distraught grandmother had buried his brother's head. She had planted the branch near the grave, but nothing had ever sprouted. But on that day, the second grandson was astonished to see that the branch had grown into a bizarre tree—leafless, but with three huge, red fruits dangling heavily and precariously from slender twigs. He reached out to pick the largest of the strange fruits. As his fingers brushed its skin, all three began to shiver and emit a low echoing tock, like the sound of the wooden bells used to pray for dead souls. Surprised, he stumbled backwards, lost his balance, and fell to the ground. Immediately, the red fruits gave one last shiver and dropped from the strange little tree, smashing against the ground in front of the terrified second grandson, like three bloody heads.

"Grandma!" he screamed, unable to rise to his feet. "Grandma, the souls of the guerillas swear they'll curse our family for the next three generations!" He rolled over and over in the grass next to the smashed fruits, howling like a mad man.

Hearing the story, everyone in the village understood that Tan Dac's sacred soul had returned to seek its revenge against the family.

Nearly another century had passed before the Cat Bac forest was declared a protected area. A paved road traversing the forest was built to accommodate the environmentalists and tourists who came to visit the preserve. As the road was being built, the workers discovered a large cave. By that time, none of the local people remembered what the cave was, nor its significance. When workers entered it, they were shocked to discover a pile of skeletons, as well as jars, pots, bronze kettles, homemade guns, swords, and lances: evidence that the guerillas had indeed died in the cave rather than surrender to the enemy.

The sacred spirits of Tan Dac and his guerillas were sealed inside that place until they rose through the soil into a strange tree with three poisonous fruits—a potent warning.

The clan of the surviving grandson, who had spied for the French, went into a steady decline from the instant that tree sprouted from the grave. It was rare for any woman in the family to give birth to a son who wasn't deformed and stillborn, or, if the child did live past birth, he always died before he was thirty. Mrs. Cay's husband was the last son of the third generation born of the mad grandson. He died when he was twenty-seven, after vomiting blood for many days.

Cuong, the hapless storage keeper at the forestry station, belonged to the fourth generation. He seemed to have finally escaped the curse that had haunted his family for so many years, but the bitter taint of so many generations of death still lingered. Cuong had been sickly since birth, not with any specific disease, but with a constant sapping illness that debilitated his manhood. By his late teens, he was only four feet, eight inches tall. On his wedding day, the photographer had to ask him to stand on a stool so he would be as tall as Tham in their wedding photograph.

Normally, it would be rare that such a man would find anyone to marry him. But Cuong lived and worked with Brigade Five, where the number of single women overwhelmed any such frivolous considerations. A debilitated man was still a man. Perhaps even more surprising though, Cuong refused to settle for a plain woman, but chose Tham, a pretty and charming young woman from Xuan Tam village, near Cat Bac township. Tham had been proud to be accepted as a worker at the forestry station, even though she hadn't come, as most of the women, from the Volunteer Youth units. As such, she had a substantial rice ration, and a decent monthly salary. To her mind, such a position was infinitely better than having to work hard year-round struggling to catch fish and rice paddy crabs in order to make a living. Because of her pride and determination, she refused all advances from passionate village men, and instead concentrated on establishing her position with the state forestry enterprise. She was content with her decision until she was transferred to Brigade Five when she was almost thirty—rather old for a single woman. It was then that she realized her position. She was getting older and the time for her to start a family was now, but here she was, isolated on this island of women.

In this environment, Cuong had the luxury of picking virtually any woman who caught his fancy when he decided to marry. Tham trembled with anger when he had named her as his choice. But what could she do? If she refused him, who could she marry? Her former admirers in the village had gone on to marry others. Most of them were fathers already, and any who remained single would have nothing to do with her, after she'd spurned their advances. If she refused Cuong, other women would rush to marry him, just for the sake of being married. Better to have a strange husband than to be an old spinster. Tham bit the bullet and accepted his offer.

It was a mistake. She soon discovered that being trapped in such a marriage was worse than being single. She and Cuong had been married for two years, and she still hadn't gotten pregnant. At first her mother-in-law, Mrs. Cay, limited herself to talking behind Tham's back. But gradually, she stopped pretending and began complaining to Tham's face.

"Ever since my son married that worthless girl," she'd yell, "the most she's been able to do is piss in a pot. She can't get pregnant!"

It was the first topic Mrs. Cay brought up whenever she met anyone. Wherever she went, she spread her poison. Her bitterness spread like the stench of shit throughout Brigade

Five; it polluted the air and suffocated Tham wherever she went. It wasn't her fault that she and Cuong were childless. She was a normal, healthy woman, absolutely capable of bearing children. It was because of Cuong she couldn't become a mother. More than once, in her anger and shame, Tham had imagined throwing herself off the island's eastern cliff.

But, also more than once, she would wonder why her mind had fixated on that side of the island.

She had begun to notice recently that the newly constructed pathway down the eastern slope had somehow changed her fellow workers . . . that somehow it seemed to have infused a sense of hope into their lives. Perhaps the secret to her own future happiness lay down that road.

She was growing more and more desperate, feeling stifled and trapped by her mother-in-law's relentless attacks. Her breaking point was finally reached on the day she heard Mrs. Cay screeching to Cuong: "I'm telling you, divorce her and marry someone else. And if you can't get permission from the authorities to do that, then find some nice, fertile woman and keep her as a mistress. Do whatever you have to do to get yourself a child!"

Tham was stunned. In spite of the virulence of her mother-in-law's attacks, she never thought the woman would advocate divorce! She was certain at first that Mrs. Cay had said such a thing just to scare her. But some time later her mother-in-law told her son she had spoken to Miss Hien from the huong nhu processing team about the possibility of an "arrangement." Another young woman's life would be ruined and Tham's life would be devastated. In her village, a divorced woman was no more than a "leftover" to be picked at by crows and vultures. She would be cursed and slandered wherever she went, forced to take the blame for everything, held up as an example of shame, and mocked without mercy. Tham imagined the village urchins chasing her, screaming at her, calling her horrible names as if she were a criminal.

The very next morning, she went to the new path and climbed down the eastern cliff. And there he was, the young man she'd heard the others whispering about for weeks. She forced herself to look at him squarely. He was the picture of the perfect man, this painter. Robust, elegant, his face handsome, seductive. She'd been forcing herself to look at her husband's monkey visage for so long that this man seemed like an angel. Wordlessly, she let him lead her to his boat, and they quickly rowed away from the island, as if they were following the steps of a choreographed dance. But just as they were about to beach at the turtle breeding camp, Tham finally spoke up.

"I can't do this now. My mother-in-law will start making noises and my colleagues will get suspicious if I'm not back soon. I just want to ask you to do me a favor."

Tuong reluctantly turned the boat around. After a few moments of uncomfortable silence, Tham again forced herself to speak. She stuttered, but went on, willing herself to take the risk, to swallow her shame in order to save herself from a worse fate—and to save her family, even though it wasn't the kind of family she had hoped for.

Tuong, for his part, was shocked at her words. They seemed more a demand than a request. Previously, the women had come to him with few words, but he had been able to understand clearly what they wanted. But this woman addressed the issue frankly, though Tuong noticed her periodic stuttering and the constant trembling of her lips as she spoke. She wanted their arrangement to be absolutely clear—like a contract. He suspected there had been some serious tragedy in her life, to make her so cautious now.

Hoa had joined him at the turtle breeding camp not long after he and Tham had made their agreement.

❧

One morning Hoa awoke to find that Tuong was gone.

Did he go fishing this early? Hoa walked to the door to peer out to sea, but instead of Tuong he saw Phuc pulling his boat onto the beach. As Phuc approached him, Hoa noticed that his friend wore his habitual gloomy scowl, almost as if he were repressing something.

"The district People's Committee and the Party Committee have requested that you come back to town with me to meet with them." A sudden sparkle flickered in Phuc's eyes. "Maybe things are looking up. Dan has been managing things with his usual inefficiency. He's nosy and fussy, like a matchmaker arriving late to an engagement ceremony. Maybe the district leaders have finally come to their senses."

Hoa climbed into the boat and returned to town with Phuc.

When Tuong returned, it was his turn to be puzzled. Where could Hoa have gone? Who came to get him? Maybe he was fed up with living here, witnessing my constant suffering and restless discontent, Tuong thought. It seemed to him that what hurt Hoa most was having a friend like Tuong who only wanted to live according to his own instincts and desires, without willpower or focus, without even the desire to build a career. He knew Hoa had hoped, had silently believed in his artistic talent. He knew Hoa had one criterion with which he evaluated anyone—either a man built himself a strong career or he didn't. In Hoa's eyes, if a person didn't subordinate himself to building a career, then that person could never be a real man.

If that were the case, then it was no surprise Hoa would get frustrated living here, was it? He had wanted to please Hoa, hadn't he? He had made a sincere effort, hadn't he? But lately he had simply surrendered any notion of self-control. His life was nothing but a vacuum of instinct and self-indulgence. He was being sucked down into a lovely but frivolous whirlpool. He could no longer distinguish all the impressions assailing him, but he knew that among the jumble of shapes and colors were white, naked legs, scattered everywhere, detached from their bodies, the faces of his decadent "artist" friends from school, the faces of girls with heavy makeup and leering smiles like Len, all tossing and tumbling together, whirling in a circle, horrifying and tantalizing him at the same time . . .

Earlier that morning, while Hoa was still asleep, he had gone once more to the eastern shore of Cat Bac. He felt certain that the woman was there, that she had been waiting for days. Sure enough, when he arrived, he found her sitting against a large rock, trying to protect herself from the chill, shivering with both cold and nervousness. He walked slowly over to her and sat down and reached for her, embracing her, drawing her to him, gently pushing his body into hers. But Tham pushed him away. "I've been waiting too long," she whispered; "I need to return now." Her voice trembled. "The day after tomorrow, I'm on night duty at the processing factory. I'll sneak over here then . . ."

And without a glance backwards, she fled.

For the next few days, Tuong was oddly restless and nervous. He was a little surprised at the nervousness. This wouldn't be his first date with a Brigade Five girl. But Hoa had come back, and Hoa was like a brake on a vehicle, like a rock in the middle of a smooth, straight road, like a stern schoolmaster with his ruler at the ready, just waiting to strike a sharp blow. How could he avoid Hoa's sharp eyes? They were able to read a person's thoughts and desires to an uncanny degree. Particularly his. So that evening, as he was getting ready to leave, he felt no great surprise when Hoa said gently: "I don't feel very well tonight, Tuong. Stay here."

Would his staying at home make Hoa feel any better? Tuong doubted it. But how could he refuse?

Around six o'clock, Hoa lay down and seemed to fall asleep almost immediately. Tuong came over and sat on the edge of the bed and looked at him. Hoa's face seemed sad and noble. Tuong thought: people don't always like him when they first meet him, but they always respect him. He studied Hoa's face, fascinated. The upper lip curled a bit, as if he were smiling at something in a dream. Then curled more, into a twist of desire. It was there, and then as quickly as it came, it was gone. The upper lip straightened, the mouth tightened into its usual resolve.

On Hoa's part, he felt as if a shadow had come to sit next to him. He sensed a cool hand on his forehead, as if someone were checking his temperature. Slowly the shadow became a beautiful girl, hovering above him. The girl from Tuong's painting, naked and lovely. She knelt by the bed and put her head on his chest and they stayed like that, in silent contentment for a long time. But then she began to grow restless, demanding, tossing and shaking her head, pleading, inciting him to act, to do something. His entire body went cold. A strong shiver started in his chest and echoed to the bottom of his feet.

He awoke with a shock to find Tuong kneeling beside his bed, his head on Hoa's chest. In the pale light cast by the kerosene lantern, Tuong's face looked sick and exhausted, as if he were the one ill, as if he were about to collapse.

"Brother Hoa," he said, "I must go."

His voice was pleading, as if he were begging Hoa for a cure. Why was he doing this? he asked himself. He could have left while Hoa was asleep. But somehow he couldn't do it, couldn't live a lie with Hoa.

A pained expression flitted across Hoa's face. He found it difficult to breathe. He turned away from Tuong and waved his hand in dismissal. Tuong's weight left the edge of his bed, and then his silent presence was hovering above him, hesitating, as if beseeching him. He said nothing. In a moment, he heard the door close softly.

He felt feverish now, not out of any sickness, but because of his dream. His body burned unbearably. Something was rising and stirring in him. A snake uncoiling. Without thinking, he jumped out of bed, threw open the door and ran like a mad man to the beach. The wind was fierce and raked so hard at his hair that he felt it was trying to yank him back and prevent him from reaching Tuong's boat. Then his feet were in the surf, just as the boat was pulling off. Wordlessly, he splashed through the water and climbed clumsily aboard.

Tuong, also silent, rowed towards the face of the cliffs. He was too shocked to say anything. Why did Hoa follow him? And how the hell would he manage it with Tham now? In the darkness, Hoa's face looked pale and placid, but he sensed a strange excitement in him, as if this were no longer the Hoa he knew. He was another person, an ordinary man with the desires that claimed most men. Hoa knew what he was up to, and he wanted to go with him. Well, why not? Why shouldn't they go together? Wasn't desire something all men shared?

As they approached the moonlit beach, Tuong said quietly, "I'll go first." He beached the boat, jumped out, and headed for the large rock at the base of the cliff.

Hoa stayed in the boat, which was still being pounded by the restless waves. His body was equally restless, but not from the tide. Eventually, he got out and pulled the boat further onto the beach and looked for a place to get out of the wind. He spotted a small pile of boulders and sheltered behind them, then lit a cigarette to calm himself down.

As he slowly inhaled the harsh tobacco, he was suddenly struck by the image of Uncle Chinh methodically preparing his bamboo whip. He began to imagine himself holding an invisible stick. He began to whittle it carefully, patiently. The rolling waves in his heart mellowed and quieted. The whirlwind in his head died down. He continued to carve his whip, as if it were the last thing he would ever do in his life. He imagined the bamboo shavings falling around him like a blessing, shining like gold. The imaginary whip in his hand was now the size of a chopstick and the fire in his heart had died down to soft embers.

The only truly happy person, at this moment, on this beach, was Tham. She had arrived an hour before. For the first time in her life, she felt the wonderful nervousness that accompanies anticipation. Although she had only seen Tuong twice in her life, she felt that somehow her heart was his. She was ashamed of her forthright demand at their first meeting. But despite her shame, a stir of love, very slight, had been awakened in her heart. She felt herself growing more and more obsessed with that seductive face she remembered.

As soon as Tuong came to her out of the darkness, she jumped at him, hugging him fiercely, kissing him all over his face. She loved him. She would meet him here whenever and however she could. Just one word from him and she would follow him anywhere in the world.

"Wait," Tuong whispered. "There is a person here who wants you very much."

"Yes, I know," Tham whispered dreamily.

They were both leaning against the rock in the moonlight.

"I mean there is . . . there is a man."

Tham stiffened. "What?"

"Sitting right over there."

Tham still didn't understand. She looked quizzically down the dark beach. "What did you say?"

But Tuong didn't dare repeat his words. His eyes probed the darkness, searching for Hoa. Tham followed his gaze. Near a pile of rocks down the beach, she thought she saw a shadow. Then the glow of a cigarette.

"Who is that?" she asked, astounded.

"He . . . he came here with me."

"What?!"

She was devastated as his meaning slowly sank in. Did he think she was nothing but entertainment? Did he think she was a whore? How could this have happened? Was this the man she had pinned all her thwarted hopes upon, the man she had sworn to devote herself to forever? She felt as if the cliff above her had suddenly fallen on her head. The waves roared and heaven, earth, and water came together in a maelstrom, as at the creation of the world. And the world was chaos. The world was a chilly and deserted place and it was void of human beings. No human beings. No more human beings. She had never felt so alone, so desperate. She turned and ran.

Tuong sat motionless for several moments after she had fled, trying to calm himself down. Finally he rose and walked heavily to the surf.

Hoa was already sitting in the rocking, buffeted boat, waiting. Despite the fierce waves, his heart was at peace. He didn't know what had passed between Tuong and Tham, nor did he grasp the reason for the sickly desperation he saw now in Tuong's eyes. He only knew that the spirit of his friend seemed to have collapsed and was lying broken inside the shell of his body. Gripping the oars firmly, Hoa rowed the boat back to their camp.

EIGHT

Once again Tuong returned to the house and found it empty. Had Phuc come again to bring Hoa back to town? He had no idea. Hoa had left without a word. He was clearly preparing for something, but what? Or was Hoa simply disgusted with him? Their personalities and values were so radically different. Could it be Hoa simply couldn't bear to be around him anymore?

The last days had been difficult. Something seemed to have broken inside himself. He had never felt self-disgust to such a degree before. Where was his life going? He thought of the people who collected the saliva of dolphins. Day after day they would row on the sea, searching for dark stains, shifting shadows on the surface of the water. If they spotted a shadow and found it was not what they thought it was, they would turn the boat and continue their search in a new direction, drifting always across the surface of the sea.

The hell with it. He would take the boat over to Cat Bac town and confront Hoa.

On his way, he ran the conversation he'd have with Hoa through his mind:

Hoa, are you disgusted with me?

Why do you ask?

Tell me the truth. If you aren't disgusted with me, then why have you been avoiding me? OK. I understand. Since that night, you see me as an unforgivable, depraved bastard. You're right—I am. I'm not worthy of your affection and support. But Hoa, I've lost everything now. Would you desert me also?

But when he arrived at the company and went into the office, he found it deserted also. Only the great turtle Phuc had killed looked at him from its glass case, stuffed and mounted and somehow naive-looking. He searched through the block of flats until at last he ran into Mrs. Nu.

"Did you come back to hear the news, Tuong?"

"What news?"

"Don't you know?!" she shouted. She leaned in close to his ear, as if she would whisper something confidential to him, but her voice rang out as loudly as it had before: "There's a meeting of the People's Committee this morning. It all seems very tense. Everybody who's not on assignment is waiting outside the gate to get the latest news. We're all hoping the district leadership will reinstate Hoa."

"Then I'll go there too. Excuse me."

He rushed to the offices of the People's Committee. As he drew closer, he saw about a dozen people walking towards him from the crossroads at the bottom of the slope. The staff of the company! In their midst was Phuc's dominant figure, and next to him was Dai, the young man he'd met on his first day. His hair was cut short now and he was clean-shaven.

"What's going on?" Tuong asked, feeling disappointed. "Is

the meeting over already?"

"Not yet, but they ordered us to disband," Phuc said, sighing. "No one knows what will happen with Hoa."

"Enough," someone said. "It won't do any good to worry now. Let's just go back and prepare for the 'democratic' meeting this afternoon."

The group, murmuring, moved to the company office. Tuong stopped and looked at the sign he had painted months ago: *Expor t Compan y, 50 Meters* . He stared at it, motionless, until Phuc came back out, took his hand, and led him gently into the office.

"The district leadership will listen to the staff's testimony this afternoon, is that it?" Tuong asked, injecting a note of cheer into his voice.

Phuc nodded silently. His face seemed more closed and secretive than ever.

❧

Phuc began his testimony slowly.

"Dear district leaders, dear company comrades. Our workers' 'democratic' discussion has gone on all afternoon. What I have to say will probably be the last thing you hear on behalf of the staff. We have heard much testimony here alleging that Mr. Hoa ran the company as a dumping place for social undesirables, as a haven for thieves, rootless drifters, people with shady pasts. In fact, I am one of those who have secrets in their pasts. So today I would like to ask your permission to tell you a few things about my life, so that you can know a little bit about the kind of person Mr. Hoa has brought to this place. I have never before told anyone these things.

"I used to be a city dweller, and I am now thirty-eight years old. In 1964, I was at conscription age, so I volunteered for the service, and was assigned to a special naval force. My training took place right on this island, and I was here for a long time. That's why, when I came to a difficult time in my life, I chose Cat Bac Island as my refuge and, with my family, decided to settle here.

"I was demobilized in 1978, and moved back to Hanoi to be a worker at the Nineteenth of August Factory.* My wife could not find a job, so every day she balanced a pole on her shoulders and wandered the streets selling noodle soup. We were poor but my family life was very stable, until one day about two years ago.

"That day I was doing some work on the side, repairing bicycles. A man, about fifty years old, brought a Mifa to my place to be repaired. I worked right outside the entrance to my collective apartment block. The work took quite a long time, since I had to rethread the chain, straighten the wheel, repair about six holes in the tire and completely reassemble the brakes. As I worked, the man spoke pleasantly to me about my family situation. Times were rough then, and I was angry because even though it was still early in the month, we'd already finished our ration of rice and the shop had refused to sell us any more until the next month. I found myself speaking to him freely about my problems, complaining about the hard

*August 19th was Victory Day in the war with the French.

conditions for workers, and blaming those in power. He sat silently, a concerned expression on his face, now and then nodding compassionately. When I'd finished speaking, he asked me if I lived in that place. Yes, I said, we lived in room 36, at the very end of the block, right near the sewage ditch.

"According to my horoscope, that year was an inauspicious one for people of my age. Let me tell you, the horoscope was right. Eventually, my customer left, and I packed up my tools and went home. About an hour later, a young man appeared at our door carrying twenty kilos of rice. He said that his 'uncle' had asked him to bring it to me. I was shocked. Thinking back, I realized that the rice must have come from my kind-hearted customer, and I didn't know what to do. I've always been rather quiet and stoic, as you know me now, but I'm easily moved, and I was very naive. I almost burst into tears, staring at that bag of rice in the middle of the floor.

"That very afternoon, the man came to our home. He glanced sympathetically around the ten square meters where my family lived. All we had for furniture was one double bed. Our clothing was hung on a rope; we had no wardrobe and no refrigerator. Bowls and plates we kept stacked on a tray in the corner, along with our two small kettles.

"The man sat without hesitation on our old bed and looked around. 'You know,' he said, 'the material life of my family is much easier than yours. But spiritually we live in a frozen void. Many times I've thought I'd rather kill myself than continue to live as I do.'

"Hearing this, a chill shot through me. I asked him why he felt that way, but he just shook his head, as if to say don't worry about me. I felt terrible that I couldn't do anything to help him. But I waited, and eventually he told me his story. Nearly twenty years before, he said, he had fallen in love with a woman. She had sworn her faithfulness, and they had gotten engaged, but before the wedding she had stolen five ounces of gold from him and then run off and married a richer man. His mother was so upset about the gold that she died half a year later. He swore he would take his revenge. Since that day he had searched for the woman, but in vain. Then about six months ago, he spotted her working in a food processing company. When she learned that he had discovered her, she took the offensive and wrote a letter to his office, accusing him of having an affair with her. She said that he had destroyed her life by getting her pregnant and then abandoning her. In addition, she accused him of stealing government property and selling it on the black market. As a result, he was severely punished—expelled from the Party and fired from his job.

"He sat there on our bed, shaking his head despairingly, his jaw clenched, but his eyes fierce and furious. At that moment I felt outraged, completely in sympathy with his anger.

"'Tell me where this damned woman is,' I said to him. 'Tell me and I'll deal with her for you.'

"He said that he wouldn't let me get involved, that she was cruel and very dangerous. But I dismissed the idea. She was after all only a woman, and I had been a specially trained commando—how could she cope with me?

"Still, he kept refusing, and I kept insisting he tell me where she was . . . as if she was my worst enemy. At last he revealed that her name was Lan and that she lived in a collective block of flats in Cau Nua. In my enthusiasm, I promised him I would shut her up for good. I was surprised at myself—except for the war, I had never even dared to think about killing another human being.

"Early the next morning, just before my wife left to sell her noodles, the man appeared at our door again. He pressed a ring worth three taels of gold into her hand. He told us that even though his family was rich, his wealth was meaningless to him. My wife and I both protested and refused over and over, but in the end we gave in to his insistence, promising ourselves we would return it one day. As soon as my wife left, he told me again not to think twice about what he called 'my small gift.' His heart would only rest easy, he said, when 'that damned witch' had been punished.

"Pausing briefly, he peered at me and asked, 'So . . . how many days do you need to eliminate her?'

"At least a week, I told him. I needed to observe her schedule and habits, to do everything carefully, so I didn't leave any trace . . .

"As I spoke, I caught a gleam of triumph in his eyes. It troubled me that his eyes seemed suddenly so cruel and strange. But at the same time I told myself that it was normal for someone who had buried that kind of hatred in his heart for so many years to have that cruelty inside himself as well.

"That evening I scouted Lan's building. The room next to hers was locked. I stopped a child who was passing by and she told me the person who lived there was a Mr. Thuoc. After the little girl left, I knocked on Lan's door and told her I was an old, long-lost friend of Mr. Thuoc and was looking for him.

She showed me his door, and I asked her when he'd be back. When she said not for a while, I asked her if I could wait in her room. She agreed. Once we were inside, I observed her carefully. She was slim and her face was very sweet, her expression clear and intelligent. She offered me tea, very hospitably, and spoke to me in a pleasant and modest way. I began to wonder how this could be the vicious, cunning woman I had heard about. I became even more perplexed when I looked around her flat. It was so much like my own—nearly empty. All her possessions could fit into two suitcases. Her son, who was about three years old, had a slight fever and was in bed in one corner of the room. After a while, she began to tell me about her life. She said she had married rather late—she was thirty-two—and she'd frequently been ill, so she and her husband thought they'd be unable to have children. But they were lucky and had a son. Unfortunately, both she and the boy were constantly sick. It seemed like every time she recovered from an illness, her son would come down with something that would put him into the emergency ward. Her husband was stationed then in the border area of Ha Giang Province, and hadn't gotten leave in over a year. They had met and fallen in love when they had both been in the war: she was in the Volunteer Youth brigades and he commanded a transportation unit. It wasn't until two years after the liberation of the South, in 1977, that they were able to reunite and marry.

"Lan's story was very simple, but I believed her. The day before, that man had touched me somehow, somewhere deep in my heart, but now I realized I didn't trust him. What I'd felt had been an emotional response, vague and unstable. Lan, however, convinced me fully. You see, those of us who have faced death constantly and survived, those of us who struggled so long on the battlefield, can understand each other very quickly. Just seeing someone walking on the street, one can feel that affinity, immediately recognize a fellow brother- or sister-in-arms.

"I stood up and told her I would go out and find some medication for her son. When I returned, I brought some herbal pills and two oranges. My gesture moved Lan deeply. She thanked me profusely and asked if I didn't want to stay and wait longer for Mr. Thuoc. I replied that I'd return the following day, and asked her not to mention anything about me to him.

"I still didn't understand what was really going on. Clearly there had to be more to the story—some shadier, hidden connection between Lan and the man.

"Late that evening, my wife came out, her shoulders sore from carrying her pole. She sat down and asked me how I managed to become friends with the director of the rice and grain company.

"'What nonsense are you talking?' I asked her.

"'You say whatever comes into your mouth,' she screamed at me, 'but whenever I have an opinion you just tell me to shut up. Go to the rice shop if you don't believe me. Ask anyone you meet if your customer isn't Mr. Dang, the director of the rice and grain company.'

"The next day I snuck into the offices of the October Rice and Grain Company to spy on Mr. Dang. And there he was, dressed in a fancy suit and tie, smiling happily, shaking hands with some visitors who had just arrived in a Toyota. He escorted them to his office, raising his eyebrows at an employee as he passed, signaling to bring refreshments. His face was no longer the face I had seen before. It was a bossy face, a tough face, a cold face. Nowhere on it could I see the suffering he'd said he'd experienced from being dismissed from the Party, from losing his job. Where, I wondered, were the signs of his collapsed spirit that had nearly driven him to suicide?

"I was terribly confused, and so for a few days I did nothing, not until Mr. Dang suddenly appeared at my door one afternoon. Once again his face was as I'd remembered it—melancholic and full of suffering. He said that for days now he'd been restless and disturbed and had thought his head would explode from the pain. If he could not take his revenge against Lan, he said, he'd have no reason to live. He urged me to 'deal with her' quickly, in the next two days. Then he put a fancy Rado watch on my wrist.

"If he'd been anyone else I would have asked him directly about his lies and stories. But standing face to face with him, I felt a chill run through me. His eyes were half-closed with supposed pain, but I felt they were cold, cruel, and sharp as a knife, and if I wasn't careful, he'd hire someone else to 'deal with' me.

"Yet I also knew I needed to find out the real story. I was certain that Lan would tell me the truth. That evening I went to her room. As soon as she saw me, she told me that Mr. Thuoc was home and I could go see him now.

"I nodded, but said: 'I'd like to talk to you for awhile first.'

"When we were seated, I immediately asked her about Mr.

Dang's personality. She stared at me, startled. 'How do you know Mr. Dang? My God, did he send you to me?'

"She was distraught, and I sensed fear and anger in her, as well as disgust. I knew I'd have to tell her the truth, or at least part of it, before she'd speak. 'He didn't send me here,' I said, 'but by chance I heard he's spoken very badly about you. I didn't want to believe what I heard, so I thought I'd ask you what the true situation was.'

"As I said before, those of us who have been in combat have a kind of veteran's sense about each other's characteristics and qualities. In short, Lan looked at me and trusted me. She buried her face in her hands for a moment, and I was briefly afraid she might collapse. But then she raised her head and looked me in the eyes and told me her story:

"'I'm the storage keeper for the October Rice and Grain Company,' she said. 'Have you seen our storage area? We keep more goods there than any other food company in the city. But my records are always clean, always in order. That's how I discovered that Mr. Dang had twice signed orders to distribute rice, but without following the proper procedures. Each time was for a dozen tons. When I asked him about the orders, and refused to release the rice for the second order, he used his authority to force me to obey. It tormented me to feel so powerless to stop him. I thought about it for a few days, tossing and turning about what to do, and then finally I met with him and told him to his face I was going to report his actions at the next company meeting. He smiled calmly and told me no one would believe me. I grew angrier and said I was going to go over his head then and report him to his superiors. That seemed to worry him, and he tried to negotiate with me, bribe me really, offering several ounces of gold as a "reward." When I refused that, he began to threaten me, telling me I'd be sorry if I said anything. That's what worries me now . . . others have been fired because they dared to disobey him, and it could happen to me too.'

"At that point, I could no longer hold my tongue: 'Don't be so simple and naive,' I said. 'If all he wanted to do was fire you, you'd be lucky . . .'

"Lan, understandably, was shocked at my words. She must have sensed my meaning though, for her face paled and when she saw someone pass by the door, she told me it was Mr. Thuoc and I should go after him.

"I told her then. 'I don't know Mr. Thuoc,' I said. 'I came here because Mr. Dang hired me to kill you.'

"Lan stared at me in horror. 'To kill me?' she whispered. 'My God, who will save me now?'

"I shook my head. 'I'm not going to do it,' I said. 'But I'm scared for my own safety. This man is extremely cruel and cunning. If I don't kill you, I'm sure he'll just hire someone else to murder both of us. I've just decided—I'm going to leave this place. And you'll have to do the same.'

"Lan gripped the edge of the table with both hands. She was trembling. 'But where will I go?'

"I asked if she had any relatives, and found out she had an aunt in Ninh Binh. I told her to start packing, but she sat motionless, as if she'd turned to stone. I was trembling myself, but I found two suitcases, threw in all her clothes and a few necessities and told her she had to get out, now.

"Poor woman—both she and the child were terrified. Her son was ill and all her energy had been sapped by fear. At the time she'd decided to stand up and struggle for what she knew was right against this man, she'd had no idea that he'd try to murder her. We hitched a ride to the outskirts of the city, and in the darkness, I flagged down a truck. I gave the driver some money and asked him to take Lan and her son someplace where they could catch another truck going to Ninh Binh.

"Then I had to think of myself and my family. Alone on that dark, empty road, I grew more and more frightened. During the war, whenever I'd go out on a reconnaissance mission, I'd never been as terrified as I was then. On missions I was active and in control. Now, I felt constantly watched, always waiting for someone to spring out of the darkness and kill me. I had no weapon, no protection. Thinking that, I stopped my bicycle, pulled my belt from my trousers, and wrapped it around the handlebars, so I could grab it quickly if I were attacked.

"When I finally got home, my wife sprang up immediately. I know all of you are familiar with her jealousy and quick temper. Well, she was furious. 'Who were you with that you're coming home this late!?' she shrieked at me.

"I didn't answer. There was no time to argue. I felt as if Mr. Dang's eyes were watching us through the bamboo curtains. Terrified, I ran to the door and looked outside. No one. I closed the door, my hand trembling, and started throwing our few belongings into one large bag.

"'Where do you think you're going—what whore are you running away with?' my wife screamed, grabbing my wrists and trying to stop me.

"I put a hand on the back of her head and the other over her mouth and pressed hard. She tried to twist away and scream. But I held her firmly and ordered her to shut up and help me pack. 'We're leaving tonight,' I said.

"As soon as she realized I wasn't going to abandon her, she calmed down. But she was still stunned at my words and stood frozen in shock. 'Move quickly,' I said, 'or I'll leave you here.'

"I said it simply to get her going, since I knew that my leaving her was what she feared most. The statement worked, but then she began to run around the room in frantic confusion, as if someone had set the house on fire. 'But I still have baskets full of noodles and soup I planned to sell to the night-shift workers,' she whined.

"I glared at her and shouted to bring them with us and sell them on the ferry.

"So we left. I carried the big bag, and my wife carried the baskets filled with noodles and soup on her strong shoulders. Our son, half-asleep, clung to his mother's basket and stumbled along behind us. We reached the harbor by five in the morning. At that time, as you know, there was no bridge to Cat Bac and people had to come by boat. By the time we reached the island, my wife had sold all her soup and noodles. We staggered into town, and I found Mrs. Mien, an old woman I'd known when I was a soldier there, and asked her if we could stay with her.

"We lived with her for six months, until I heard that the export company was recruiting people who knew how to work on the water. I'd heard rumors that the director hired people based on their demeanor and his own instincts, with no questions about their pasts. When I met him, I found that the rumors were true. Mr. Hoa hired both my wife and me as contract workers until we were registered as new residents. Then, when the company built new housing, we were given a flat as well.

"Today is the first time my wife has heard this story. I know that many times during the past two years, she wanted to ask me what had happened, but she was afraid of my temper and, I think, afraid to know what I had done. A few months ago, however, she read in the newspaper that a man named Quach Tien Dang had been arrested and was being put on trial. She rushed to me with the news, saying, 'That man Dang you were so secretive about is in jail on charges of corruption and threatening his workers. Do you have anything to do with this? That night you forced us to flee, I knew something had happened. I was afraid you might have robbed or murdered someone . . .'

"Once again I had to roar to shut her up. But now, my wife, you know my secrets. And comrades, you also now know the truth about a man you suspected of some darkness in his past. There is more than one person here with secrets, and I hope that now they too will feel confident and comfortable enough to share them one day.

"I am telling you all this because I want to show you an example of the kind of person to whom Mr. Hoa has given a second chance, and to state, on my honor, that Mr. Hoa is a decent man without a speck of dirt on his hands. I am sure every worker here would say the same. As for his business and management skills—I don't need to go into that. The company books and the annual report speak for themselves.

"Thank you for listening to me, dear comrades!"

❧

A week after the meeting, Hoa was reinstated as director. He had the support of several powerful members of both the People's Committee and the Party Committee. But, as Phuc had noted, the most convincing evidence in his favor was the success the company had achieved during his tenure.

Tuong was happy for Hoa, but he couldn't overcome his own feelings of sadness. One day, not long before Hoa's reinstatement, he bluntly asked the director if he were going to fire him.

Hoa looked surprised. "Why would I fire you? There's no question of that. But I'll tell you something, Tuong. I need to get back to the company. I can't take staying away much longer."

Saying these words aloud, hearing himself speak them, Hoa came to realize something about himself. This need he had to prove himself to everyone was strong, perhaps his strongest characteristic. People who didn't understand him would say—or think—he had no human desires or needs. It wasn't true; he knew that. But all his drive had been subordinated to the desire to prove to everyone his competency and his abundant capacity for work. That was the pride that pushed him. During the time he'd spent now at the turtle breeding camp, that desire had burned even more deeply in his heart, and now it informed him completely. He recognized and accepted this about himself. But shouldn't he have known that all human beings have different needs, desires? Wasn't it utopian to believe one could eliminate them fully? Had he been wrong in pressing Tuong to eliminate what he had been so thirsty for? But couldn't human beings control those instincts, rather than try to deny them?

Once he returned to the company, he was loaded down with work, and he no longer had time for all of these thoughts. Only sometimes, at night, when he returned to his room and saw the sign marked *Bac helors* that Tuong had painted so long ago, would he feel a creeping sense of emptiness. Could it be he didn't handle Tuong as he should have? Perhaps it would be better to bring him back to the mainland and try to help him.

Two days later, as Hoa was checking the books, Phuc entered the room tentatively. Since his confession to his wife and co-workers, his face had lightened considerably. But at that moment Hoa could see lines of worry and concern etched onto his forehead. Phuc sat down heavily.

"Hoa," he said, "I have to tell you I'm really disappointed in Tuong."

"What? What happened to him?" Hoa struggled to contain his anxiety.

"He's always disappearing from the turtle breeding camp. No one knows where he goes. Sometimes I've had to go look after the turtles myself—I haven't told you that."

Hoa tried to stay calm. "I want you to tell him to come

back here and meet with me. We're going to close that camp anyway."

Tuong sat face to face with a silent Hoa. He was certain he was about to be chewed out for abandoning the camp too often.

"Brother Hoa," he began, his voice catching. He glanced out of the window, to the bay beyond. Several boats were gliding past, searching for dolphin saliva. It was difficult for him to speak. "Please," he said finally, "don't feel you have any obligation to me whatsoever. Don't try to be my savior anymore. I'm hopeless and decadent."

Hoa's voice was calm but his emotions were intense.

"Don't speak like that. We're still brothers, just as we always have been." He decided to change the subject, distract Tuong. "I'm bringing you back here to take charge of the company's books again. You don't have to return to the turtle camp. We've done enough studies and experiments on them; we have the information we need on their living habits, their methods of reproduction, and their relationship to the environment. I'm preparing a plan that will allow us to preserve a large-scale area for turtle breeding. The district leaders like the idea . . . Tuong, in short you won't have to live in that lonely place anymore."

As he listened to Hoa speak about the camp, Tuong felt a scramble of panic. After Hoa's reinstatement, Tuong had grown even more distraught and confused. He'd grown used to having someone there, and then, suddenly, he was alone. He'd felt abandoned, isolated from all normal human contact. He'd thought of Hoa, involved again in his career. Everyone Tuong knew had duties, responsibilities, challenges, passions. They were involved in work and life. Only he had been left by the wayside. He was twenty-four years old and what the hell did he have to show for it? In his sadness and desperation, he returned often to the secret beach, where the middle-aged women waited for him . . .

"Please don't protect me anymore," he blurted. "People will spread rumors—I'm the proof they need to condemn your hiring practices. I'll just be more ammunition for them to use against you." He had sat up straight in his chair, his body tense, as if he were begging. He began to rise.

Hoa laughed and pushed him back down. "Don't be ridiculous. Do you think after I've coped with all these challenges, faced down all their cruel slanders, that I'd abandon you now?" He shook Tuong gently, then released his shoulders and smiled. "By the way, did you know the women in the national park area are going to be reassigned to the mainland? A regiment of demobilized soldiers is coming in to replace them." He smiled. "Excuse me for a moment, Tuong. I have to be somewhere."

When he'd gone, Tuong spotted a letter on his desk. It was from Van. Her familiar handwriting stabbed him with shame: he felt unworthy to touch the pure white envelope. Oh, Van . . .

A sudden shrieking noise brought him to his feet. He went over to the window. A white ambulance with a whirling red light on top rushed through the gate of the hospital on the other side of the road. It screeched to a halt and stretcher bearers in white scrubs ran to it and began unloading injured people.

He walked over to the hospital and asked a bystander what had happened. "There was an accident near the Bua Gorge. A transport van was coming down the slope when the driver realized his brakes weren't working. Some of the passengers got so frightened that they jumped out before it stopped. People had their heads split open, arms and legs broken . . ." The man suddenly seemed angry. "What the hell kind of driver goes into the mountains without checking his brakes?"

The injured lay on the stretchers, their blood reddening the white canvas. Tuong looked up to the mountains, towards the village that housed Brigade Five. But he couldn't see anything behind the mist hanging over the jungle. Staring at that white shroud, he remembered Hoa telling him that the women in the state forestry enterprise would be replaced by male soldiers.

And in the wind blowing down to him from the mountains now, he heard the echo of horses' hooves, the sound of Tan Dac's soldiers coming back, moving swiftly through the jungle of jackfruit trees and bamboo.

ABOUT THE AUTHOR AND THE TRANSLATORS

HO ANH THAI is one of the most prolific writers in Vietnam. He belongs to the generation of writers who came of age after the war with America. He began writing in 1977 at the age of seventeen and has since published fifteen novels and short story collections. Several of his stories have been translated into English and published as *Behind the Red Mist: Short Fiction by Ho Anh Thai*. He completed an M.A. and Ph.D. while living in India, and now works for the Ministry of Foreign Affairs in Hanoi.

PHAN THANH HAO lives in Hanoi. She is the Assistant Editor-in-Chief of *Education and Times,* published by the Ministry of Education and Communication. She has translated *The Class* by Eric Segal and *Evening News* by Arthur Hailey into Vietnamese, and she is the first translator of Bao Ninh's novel *The Sorrow of War,* published in England and the United States. She was the chief consultant for *Even the Women Must Fight: Memories of War from North Vietnam,* by Karen Gottschang Turner. Her poetry appears in the anthology *Visions of War/Dreams of Peace,* and her short stories have been published in Australia.

CELESTE BACCHI lived in Hanoi for seven months while assisting on this book. With Phan Thanh Hao she has edited and translated numerous short stories and essays. Bacchi also worked as both an English and a kindergarten teacher during her time in Vietnam, South Asia, and Europe. She currently resides in San Francisco, where she is a law student focusing on international human rights law.

WAYNE KARLIN is professor of language and literature at the College of Southern Maryland, and directs the fiction program for the annual Literary Festival at St. Mary's College of Maryland. He served in the Marine Corps in Vietnam. In 1973 he contributed to and co-edited the first anthology of fiction by Vietnam veterans, *Free Fire Zone.* In 1995 he did the same for *The Other Side of Heaven: Postwar Fiction by Vietnamese and American Writers,* with Le Minh Khue and Truong Vu, an anthology that includes editors, writers, and stories from all sides of the war. With Ho Anh Thai, he also co-edited a collection of contemporary American short fiction that was published in Vietnam in 1998. He edited and worked on the translations of *The Stars, the Earth, the River: Fiction by Le Minh Khue, Behind the Red Mist: Fiction by Ho Anh Thai,* and *Against the Flood* by Ma Von Khang.